Burke's

Burke's Last Witness

By

CJ Dunford

Fahrenheit Press

For The Cast (Andrew Hainey, Mark Kydd, Gregor Firth) and

director (Stuart Nicol) of Burke and Al 'the man in the pub' Guthrie

I

Wind whipped across the execution site. Hugh Rose's outlook from the platform across the Lawnmarket was dizzying. From the five-storey tenements on both sides every window was open and out of them hung four or more people apiece, yelling and waving their hats. The rumours that people were making money from the execution by selling viewing space was obviously true. At their back loomed the foreboding shadow of St Giles Cathedral, a silent witness to much of the city's bloodshed and death, but in his imagination dark and sternly disapproving. The crowd below ranged from the Lawnmarket, up the castle and down towards to the Port of Leith, packed densely together and all baying, like wild beasts, for death. In all his career Rose had never witnessed such a spectacle of combined hate and unbridled joy. Despite the close proximity of those on the platform he felt cold deep down inside him. This was the nineteenth century, the age of civilisation, and yet the people of his city massed together like some great monster sent by Satan himself to drag one soul down into hell.

Snow began to fall across his vision, light and swift, but he could still make out the once handsome face of the man who stood in front of him. Dirty, unshaven, with his lank dark locks falling below the collar of his ill-fitting black suit, the prisoner still held himself with a vestige of his former confidence. His blue eyes met Rose's directly and the condemned man gave a partial wink, so quick only Rose could see it. As he did the laughter lines flashed across his face. Rose knew him well enough to know he revelled in the attention. A lesser man would have quailed before the hate of an entire city, but William Burke, accused of being the most notorious serial killer the country had ever caught, relished his last moment of life. A memory flashed into Rose's mind of the first time his men dealt roughly with him. Burke had urged them to 'take care with such a historical figure'. Whatever he was and whatever he'd done, Rose saw an extraordinary bravery in this man and it made him doubt. Doubt everything.

Rose dropped his gaze to the wooden platform beneath him; the normally grubby planks scrubbed clean for the great occasion. Below this the crowd roared. He could make out words like 'murderer', 'death' and all the usual abuse thrown at the condemned. The difference was the volume. A sea of humanity surged below them. Doubtless the pickpockets and ruffians were having a fine time. But Rose envied his men down there in the thick of it all struggling to keep the peace. Up here, wedged between the many clergymen Burke had invited to witness his death, it was warmer and ranker. He stood so close to the priest on his left he could see the sweat breaking out on his fat face and had all too good a view of the large black pockmarks that littered his skin.

The priest who was muttering, intoning liturgy Rose guessed, had a small smug smile lifting the corner of his mouth, obviously proud of gaining his place in history.

The hangman, an over-muscled, toothless individual, chosen for his ability to repel climbers onto the scaffold and for his apparent complete lack of compassion for his victims, pushed forward and lowered the rope around Burke's neck.

The wind changed direction and Rose felt his eyes begin to sting as the snow was driven directly at the little group. He brushed it from his eyelashes to watch Burke's last moments as he had promised. Burke's gaze met his and then the condemned man spoke, but the wind whipped away the words.

'I can't hear you,' shouted Rose.

Burke mouthed the words again.

Suddenly, Rose knew it was vital he heard what Burke was trying to tell him. Only then would he understand. He pushed one priest aside and then another. The more he pushed towards Burke the further he seemed to be from him. He pushed yet another priest and this one fell, plunging off the platform, his black tunic billowing in the wind like a giant crow.

'Stop,' shouted Rose, 'this is not right. The truth has not been told.' He began to push with a frenzy that both sprang unbidden from within and yet was somehow without. He felt his hand lash out and contact with each rough, dark cloak; the shock of impact followed by a cry as his victim fell. He was knocking men to their death. He knew it, but again and again his arm lashed out and struck another.

The crowds below buffeted the pillars of the platform. A man grabbed the nearest pole and began to climb. Others followed. In a moment the platform would be overrun. The hangman jumped and was swallowed by the crowd below.

Burke grinned, showing perfect teeth. He spoke again and this time Rose heard him. 'Time to wake up, matey.'

'Hugh! Hugh! Wake up!'

Hugh Rose struggled through layers of sleep towards the sound of his wife's voice. The warmth of the bed could not stop his teeth chattering. His whole body shook. He dry-wretched, disorientated and disturbed.

'Hugh! Hugh! I need you!'

'What's wrong?' He pushed himself up to a sitting position and the rough blankets fell away. Sweet Jesus, but it was cold! It must still be the middle of the night. He blinked, straining to see through the pitch dark. His thin nightshirt offered little protection from the winter winds that swept through the ragged wooden shutters. A nightmare. It was only a nightmare. He would never – how could he even imagine he would…

'Hugh!'

He swung his feet onto the floor, wincing in pain at the

freezing touch of the stone and groped his way towards his wife, Sarah. His fingers found her sitting by the foot of their bed, rocking. One of the children was in her arms.

'No, not the babe!'

'No, Hugh. James and Ben are both sleeping sound. It's Jenny. She's on fire.'

Hugh rubbed his eyes and managed to make out the outline of the sweet face of his seven-year-old daughter. Tentatively he put out his hand and touched her forehead. He jerked his hand back unable to believe the heat that stung his fingers. 'I'll get the doctor.'

'We can't afford it.'

'I don't care about the cost.' Hugh felt his way to the fire and stirred the coals. An ember flickered. He lit a rushlight from it and carried it carefully to the oil lamp. Shadows flickered over the bedroom where all the family slept. James was sound in his cot and Ben, his older brother, curled in the little space under the shutters, close to the fire.

'Them doctors ain't interested in the living. As you well know. Get Mary from the fourth floor. She's reared fifteen children successfully. I'd rather her advice than theirs.'

'I'll take her through to the other room. No point waking the children.' He lifted his fragile daughter from his wife's arms. 'I think Mary will likely take more kindly to you chapping her door than me.'

Mary, a hag in her mid-forties with rat-tail hair and worn out by childbearing, soon appeared with his wife. They chased him from the room despite his protests. 'Sickrooms ain't no place for men. More useless there than anywhere and that's saying something,' she spat at him through blackened teeth.

Rose paced in the bedroom till daylight. Sarah didn't come. At last he dressed himself in his uniform and roused the boys. They blinked at him with their wide blue eyes, tousle-haired and sleepy. He fed them a thin gruel he heated over the fire. James, not quite yet two years old, sat on his lap and snuggled in tight. Rose absentmindedly stroked his hair. He couldn't bring himself to eat. Both boys were unusually subdued. Finally Sarah beckoned from the door. He put James down in his chair and tucked a blanket around him. A stern look sufficed to tell his brother to take care of him. He went over to Sarah and spoke in a low voice. 'How is she?'

'The fever's broken.'

'Thank God for that,' said Hugh.

Sarah shook her head. 'Don't be thanking God yet, Hugh. She fitted half the night away.'

'What! You should have let me get a doctor.'

'And what would he have done that Mary and I could not? We cooled her. Stopped her from hurting herself. There was nothing else to be done. She'd not have kept anything in her stomach.'

Rose passed a weary hand across his eyes. 'Yes. You're right, of course. I did not mean to speak in anger. It's just she's my,' his voice broke roughly, 'little angel.'

Sarah laid her hand on his arm. 'I know my love.' She bit her lip. 'I've argued with myself whether or not to tell you this, but I've decided you should be warned.'

'Warned?'

'Mary says – because of the fits – she may be changed.'

'Changed how?'

'The heat may have got into her brain. It may have stolen some of her wits.'

Rose could find no words. He flung open the door and stepped out. Behind him he could hear the quiet sound of Sarah beginning to weep and wee Jamie querulously demanding what was wrong. He shut the door behind him and strode out for the gaol.

It was not yet full light, but the streets were already busy with hawkers, opening up their shanty stalls around St Giles and down the Royal Mile. Old women, bent almost double by baskets as large as a ten-year-old child and piled high with fish, jogged past him. Each eager to reach the fish sellers first with the catch of the morning off the boats in Leith. The water men in their city blue uniforms were hustling back and forth with buckets to serve the rich. Barefoot children scampered between them with small jugs, eager to pinch a penny or two of their trade. Above the street, windows were opening in all floors of the tall tenements as people gave a perfunctory yell and chucked their night soil out to road below. The smell was unpleasant but Rose, who had once had the misfortune to visit York, was glad of the comparatively wide streets between the tenements which allowed the effluence to run in rivers down the sides of the cobbles. The sharp cold stole much of the smell. Most mornings he revelled in the busy bustle of the city before he plunged into the gloom of the gaol where he must spend much of this day. But this morning he barely saw the scene around him. Fortunately, his tall, wiry figure, stern square face with its soldier's crop and the uniform of the Captain of the Guard carved a path for him through the city's street.

The gaol, with its mismatched roof outline, could have passed for quaint if you didn't know what went on inside its walls and how often the last glimpse of blue sky those incarcerated there would ever see was when they danced on the end of a rope for the crowd's amusement.

Rose stepped over the threshold of the large studded wooden doors. The entrance was slightly less cold as the two guards had a meagre fire burning, but the smell of damp and mould already lingered in the air. He nodded at the men on guard. 'Still alive, is he?'

There were at this time thirty-three souls in the gaol, but neither man had any doubt who he meant. 'Yes, more's the pity,' said the older, grizzled man and spat into the fire making it hiss.

'Yes, devil take him,' echoed the younger, a lad of no more than nineteen summers. His eyes darted back and forth as if he expected the devil to arrive at any moment.

'I'm going in. Unlock it.'

The younger guard hurried to open the outer gate. Hugh

held keys for all the cells within, but as a matter of caution only the guards at the door held the keys to the final gate. All the guards went armed and most of them, certainly the ones who went down to the depths, were battle-hardened fighters but, still, being in this gaol made every man and woman desperate and frightened. Fear of death could lend a surprising strength to even the weakest. When you had nothing left to lose, what was the death of a guard or two? And if you died in the attempt, it was a quicker and cleaner death than dancing on the end of a rope.

Burke was being kept on the lowest level of the prison. At the foot of the steps of the second stage, Rose lit a primitive horn lantern. After years working here he knew his way around blind, but he wanted to see Burke's face. He also knew that the lowest inmates were not above throwing their faeces at him and, while the light made him a target, he could identify the troublemaker and send a man or two in to have a quiet chat with the miscreant to make him rethink his ways.

Finally, he came to the door to Burke's cell. To his annoyance, he found his hand shaking as he slipped the large key into the lock. The iron-reinforced door creaked open. Rose held his lantern aloft. Water ran down the walls in tiny rivulets. The cell smelled of a mixture of stagnant pond and shit. Burke was lying on a bundle of straw he had scraped together. He muttered and twisted but his eyes were closed. Rose closed and locked the door behind him. He edged forward, his hand on his sword. Burke moaned again. Rose kicked out with his boot, connecting hard against Burke's ribs and sending the man rolling off his straw into the filth of the floor.

The light struck him full in the face as he rolled away. Burke put up a hand, half in protest, half in surrender. His thick brown hair was tangled and his face grimy. He blinked and opened his blue eyes wide. A smile flashed across his even features.

'Alright Captain, alright. I was dreaming. And I'm to be thanking you for waking me. If these are to be my last few hours on earth I'd rather not spend them in nightmares.'

'Then I'm sorry I woke you.'

'Ah Captain, don't be like that. Welcome to my cell. If I had more than water I'd offer it to you, but, wait a minute, I've a mite of bread left. I do believe that bit wiggled. I'll give you the meaty bit by way of friendship.'

'You disgust me.'

'And yet you're here. Surely a captain has better ways to spend his time than sitting with the most notorious killer Scotland has ever seen?'

Before either man was fully aware of what was happening, Rose hauled Burke to his feet and thrust him hard against the wall, his face inches from Burke's. 'What manner of creature are you?'

Burke held his gaze for a moment. He placed his hands over Rose's taking care not to grip them. He spoke softly. 'Easy, man, easy. You'll not be wanting to cheat the crowd of its spectacle. To say nothing of ending a career in ignominy.' He gave Rose a friendly wink. The captain let go abruptly, dropping Burke to the floor.

Rose stormed from the cell. 'Watch him,' he yelled spitefully at a guard. 'He means to destroy himself.' He didn't stop to hear the guard's reply. He fairly ran up the steps and pounded on the final gate as if the hounds of hell were at his heels. He needed to feel the sun on his face. He'd have to go back. He didn't need to visit Burke again today, only hear the reports. But Burke's face hovered in his mind's eye – that strange half-wink he had given him just now, an uncomfortable echo of his dream last night. All Rose's instincts told him something was very wrong and the best thing he could do was stay away from the man.

Being the captain gave him some leeway to leave the gaol and survey the city, arguing that his presence sent a warning to be would-be miscreants, but duty if nothing else would soon turn his footsteps back the way he had come. The high street had settled now into its regular bustle. The chaos of first light was over. The stalls around the cathedral were open. Their raised roofs now displaying a variety of wares from the new and shiny cloak pins to the second-hand socks stolen from the dead and sold to the poorest on the street. Vagrant dogs that roamed free at night now slunk into doorways, wary of the traders who mercilessly kicked them away from their stalls in case they frightened off potential buyers.

A young scallywag, no more than eight years old, his feet wrapped in toe-rags, sidled up to the stall selling socks, caught Rose's eye and ducked back into the shadows. Rose nodded approvingly. Although his superiors disagreed, Rose strongly believed that preventing crime was the future of the city guard. He was fully aware that others saw them merely as hired thugs, who would beat a criminal half to death in the depths of the gaol and then send him on his way to warn his friends not to cross the law. But surely, Rose thought, it was better to have a presence on the street and make those, like that young boy, think again about stealing. In his mind he heard Sarah laugh at his opinion. She had come from a poor and large family and he knew she had worked from childhood to support them. He had never asked what she had had to do to put a crust on her parents' table, but he suspected. She was desperate that their children had a good start in life. 'I don't want my children to do what I had to do to survive,' she'd say to him a dozen times a week. 'It's not the evil that sink to crime it's the desperate. For some there is no other way.' What had she been forced to do, his bonnie Sarah, before she'd met the handsome young guard in The Last Drop and he'd swept her away to a new life? Sometimes when she didn't realise he was watching her, he'd see the shadows slide over her face, the memories of those dark times. He was aware of a sudden impulse to buy the urchin his socks, but curbed it. The boy was not his responsibility and he had little enough money to protect his own.

But the train of thought stuck with him as he made his way back to the gaol. Unbeknown to him he scowled ferociously when puzzling over any dilemma and several would-be thieves seeing him decided they could spend the day without their coveted items.

Rose stepped back into the shadows of the gaol. 'What cell have they put Hare in?' he asked the watch guards. The words were out of his mouth before he had realised what he meant to do.

II

Turning King's evidence had given Hare some advantages. His cell, though rank and rat- and flea-infested, had a barred window from which came natural light shattering the dark gloominess of the cell. The straw, also, had been changed in living memory. The man sat up and rubbed his eyes as Rose entered. 'Morning, Your Honour. Have you come to set me free?'

'Not yet,' answered Rose. The stench in Hare's cell was far worse than Burke's. Rose's eyes caught the sight of an over-flowing bucket in the corner.

'Your Honour's food is not quite agreeing with me,' said Hare.

Rose suppressed a desire to gag with difficulty. It didn't help that Hare was as ugly as one of Hell's denizens. There was little symmetry in his face. His nose, broken once too often in a fight, seemed to twist left then right then left again. His teeth were blacked stumps with one or two snaggly white teeth hanging on beyond reason. His eyes seemed to retreat into their sockets and lie there black as pitch. He was stockily-formed and, though not tall, gave the impression that in a fight he would be low and vicious. In all ways he was the opposite of the charming and charismatic Burke. It was all too easy to believe that Hare was a vicious killer, and yet he would be the one to go free.

'Begging Your Honour's pardon, but I've been in here a mighty long time and being as I'm now a law-abiding citizen again, it don't seem quite right I'm shut up in gaol with all these villains.'

'There's been a subscription set up to help Daft Jamie's mother bring a private case against you.'

Hare tilted his head to one side and blinked owlishly. 'I don't understand, Your Honour. I did my duty, though it made my heart sore.'

Rose's hands curled themselves into fists. He took a deep breath and stilled himself. No stranger to violence, the longer his career in the gaol continued the more he tried to distance himself from those within it. I am a reasoning man, he told himself. Lashing out at this poor specimen of humanity would make me no better than he. When I have finished with him I will lock the door and leave him here in his filth while I can walk free in the sunlight. That is punishment enough. But in his heart of hearts he knew it was not. Burke's helpmate had escaped the noose by turning King's evidence and convicting his partner. He too was responsible for the hideous catalogue of deaths the two had inflicted and it made no sense to Rose that this rogue should go free because he was the quicker to turn on his associate. If anything it made him loathe the man even more. There is no honour among the poor and desperate his Sarah often told him, but these men were something worse. Something vile. Something unheard of in their callous and carefree slaughter.

'I've been talking to Burke,' said Rose. Again the words were out before he knew it and as he spoke them he realised it had been his intent all along to discuss Burke with this wretch.

'Sure, he was the best man a friend could have,' said Hare. 'He'd give you the coat off his back.'

'And this is how you repay his friendship,' sneered Rose, but Hare seemed not to hear him.

'Everyone liked William. Life and soul of any party. When he had a penny or two to spare he'd get up these little parties for the local children.'

'Good God,' broke in Rose, aghast. 'Are you telling me…?'

Hare shook his head, his face sorrowful. 'No. No, Your Honour. He never harmed a hair on their heads. He liked kids. He was a kind man. He is a kind man.'

'How can you say that?'

Hare shrugged. 'It all crept up on us, Your Honour. And the money was very tempting to ones as poor as us.'

The man's a fool thought Rose. No wits in his head to understand what he has done. But he asked anyway, 'Whose idea was it?'

'William's.' Hare answered without hesitation.

'You claim to have been a god-fearing man,' said Rose. 'Did you never question him?'

Hare stood and met him eye to eye. 'I trusted him. He always saw me right.' He held Rose's eye for several heartbeats. Rose, who had seen the horrors of the battlefield, felt a shiver run down his spine. There was something unspoken here. Something that was passing him by. Then Hare turned and slumped back down in a corner. 'If I'm not to be freed today, Your Honour, could you see yourself right to speaking to the cook about my food? Whatever they're putting in it it's making my stomach right sore. You've got to feel sorry at least for the boy who will be taking the slops out.'

'Who said anyone will?' said Rose over his shoulder as he left.

Hare gasped. 'Yer cannot leave me without facilities,' he said.

Rose shrugged in return and locked the door behind him. It was a petty victory and left a taste of bile in his throat. Or maybe that was just the smell of Hare and his bucket. He'd have to speak to the guards, who were no doubt pissing in his food. He doubted he could face that smell again and already he knew he would be returning.

That night Rose returned home to rooms that had been scrubbed to within an inch of their lives. An aroma of meaty broth met him as he opened the front door. His eyes took in the neatness of the room, Ben and Jamie both with freshly-washed faces playing together, strangely quiet in the corner with their wooden horses which he roughly-carved last Christmas, everything in its place. As he closed the door his little sons looked up but did not run to him as usual, their blue eyes wary. Sarah came through from the bedroom and flung her arms around his neck. 'Is Jenny no better, love?' he asked, already knowing the answer.

'She sleeps,' said Sarah. 'The boys are being very good and quiet so she can mend the quicker.'

Rose released his wife and bent down to hug his sons. 'Good boys,' he said. They both snuggled in to him without a word. God, if even the children sensed how ill she was it must be bad, he thought. 'The place is looking grand, Sarah.'

'I thought I'd get it all in order for when Jenny wakes,' said Sarah. 'We're always in such a mess in these twa rooms I thought it would be nice for her to see them tidy.' She smiled at him, blinking back a tear, and Rose knew that Sarah was trying to control all she could while the life and wellbeing of her daughter was held solely in the Lord's hands. 'When you're made governor,' she began, but the old joke between them was too thin for comfort.

Rose seized her again in a bear hug. 'I've had a long hard day at work and I want some of that wonderful stew. Don't you boys? I'm as a hungry as a bear. What about you cubs?' Jamie and Ben growled playfully and he tumbled round the room with them while Sarah set the table. He noticed she didn't set a place for herself.

'I'm going through to see if she'll take a wee bit,' she said.

Rose nodded. 'I'll sleep through here in front of the fire tonight with the boys. You and Jenny take the bed.' Sarah nodded although he knew she had decided that long before he had come home. Still, sleeping on a rough floor under a roof was a much lesser hardship than he had endured as a soldier. Moreover he would be able to hear his two little men breathing through the night and ensure they had taken no ill from their older sister.

III

The morning saw Jenny no better and no worse. She slept on. Sarah had decided this was a healing sleep but on his way out Rose ran across Mary. He thanked her for her help with Jenny. She acknowledged his thanks, but would not look him in the eye. It was with a heavy heart and a mind full of doubt that he made his way to the gaol.

The morning was much as it had been yesterday and the day before. Rose knew as he watched a fisherwife run by, the basket on her back filled with fish so heavy she was nearly bent double, that for her the day had begun before dawn as she had carried an even heavier load out to the boat. It was essential her husband didn't get his feet wet, so she carried him. He probably smelled no different from the fish he caught. These women always with a fishy burden on their back. Always running. For the tide. To be the first in market. They passed him every morning and it struck him for the first time that they must be in pain, but a pain so familiar and usual that perhaps their bodies no longer noticed it. Whereas his burdens – his worry for Jenny, this nagging feeling that something about Burke was awry, his duty to keep the town peaceful, to protect his family – his burdens were as invisible as they were heavy. Normally he too felt numbed by what he must carry day to day, but Jenny's illness had brought a sudden awareness and life felt raw, painful and all too precious this morning.

That a man could kill so many and still smile.

He greeted the guards curtly. 'I must check he has no new plans of self-murder,' he said. Keys were produced. They knew even without Rose naming him the prisoner he meant to see. He took a stool from the guardroom even though this was forbidden.

This time Burke greeted him with a cheery babble. 'Hallo! You missed the party, Captain. Draw up a pew. I see you've brought your own. I'll tell you what you missed. Two priests this morning. One before dawn. Both ready and eager to hear my confession. And that one man who stood watching me all night, poor fellow. Apparently, there'd been a rumour spread I meant to destroy myself and cheat the gallows. As if I would. For that is a mortal sin!'

Rose half-listened, his eyes surveying the tiny cell. Fresh straw lay on the floor and the slop bucket was fresh and clean.

'Ah, I see you are admiring my clean premises,' said Burke with a proprietary grin. 'The guard on night duty was persuaded it would assail both our noses less if my cell was cleaner.'

Rose made a noise of disgust that sounded like 'Pah!'

'Sure, your guards are right good men. Once we'd got over the introductory beatings we've settled down into a good relationship. For aren't we all men in the eyes of God?'

'What kind of creature, are you?' spat Rose. 'You talk of priests and confessions! As if one so mired in evil can understand the nature of sin.'

Burke sat up rubbing his hands in glee. 'A theosophical debate! You are a rare man, Captain. Rare indeed. And so am I. I am as well versed, if not more so, in the scriptures as you. Was I not the most regular attendant of the Sabbath evening meetings in the Grassmarket? And was I not among the loudest to lament their loss?'

'The priests may believe you sincere in your desire for redemption, but I am not so blind. I have never met a creature so vile, so depraved, so...so... You leave me speechless.'

'Not obviously so.'

Rose was across the floor before he knew it. His hands

curled against the lapels of Burke's collar as he thrust him against the damp stone wall.

'Easy. Easy man. You've a right temper on you. Or is it a bad day you're having?'

Disgusted with himself, Rose let Burke go. He picked up a handful of fresh straw and wiped his hands on it. His gesture was lost on Burke, who was twisted round and pulling at his coat.

'Look what you've done to my collar!' Burke exclaimed. 'Not that it was that fine, if I'm honest. If only that cheating rascal Bill Hare would give me my due I'd be able to make a creditable last appearance.'

Rose sank down on his stool. He was aware of a bubble of laughter within him. He fought it down, managing to say only, 'You're worried for your appearance?'

Burke did his best to brush himself down. 'I'm certain of a good crowd,' he said. 'I should look my best. Sure, it'll be a fine outing for the good folk of this city.'

Rose rubbed a hand over his face.

Burke's voice broke through his confusion, 'I puzzle you, don't I Captain? And yet you do not leave. Why I believe you'd like to make a study of me!'

Rose looked up. 'I've been to see Hare. He says it was all your idea.'

Burke chuckled. 'He'd be a fool to say aught else now, wouldn't he.'

'Then tell me. Whose idea was it? Yours or Hare's?' he asked bluntly.

'You want to hear the truth?'

'Are you capable of telling it?'

Burke pulled together some straw and sat down, flicking his coat out from under him. 'I've been told I tell a yarn well. Make yourself comfy Captain Rose and I'll tell you how it all began, but I warn you, you won't like what you hear.'

As Burke began to speak the story unfolded in Rose's mind's eye.

Hare's lodging house was rough. Families slept in shifts in the two dirty rooms. It was the only way to make enough money to satisfy the landlord. Hare might be the nominal landlord, but he had another master to answer to. The man they rarely saw, who came only to collect the money or more often sent a servant into the filth of the Old Town in his lieu. Hare and Burke and their women had the best beds but that was saying little and even theirs were slept in by others. The rooms were always dark and always frowsy with the smell of unwashed flesh and old men farting in their sleep. This morning Burke was sitting before the unlit fire nursing a headache fit to burst his skull when Hare crouched down beside him in a rare state.

'The bugger's gone and died on me, William. And him still owing the rent!' He jerked his head back towards the major's bed where the old man lay still as stone.

Burke rubbed his temples with his fingers, trying to take in what his friend was saying. 'Is it bad, Bill?' he asked. His tongue felt like a dried turd.

'Bad enough,' said Hare. 'The landlord's not the forgiving kind.'

Burke felt a desperate, familiar desire for whisky, which he knew he'd have to slake before long. 'What are you going to do?' he asked thickly.

Hare beat his fist against his other palm. 'I don't know,' he snapped. 'You're the one with the brains, William. What can I do?'

Whisky. He wanted whisky. 'You mean how do you get a dead man to pay up?' he said, attempting to feel his way around the problem and finding no answer.

Hare sat back on his heels and gave a low whistle. 'Now there's a thought. He'd be worth money to some.'

Burke's head jerked up. Pain lanced through his temples. 'I didn't mean…' he began, but was unable to complete the sentence as horror and pain distracted him.

Hare patted him on the arm. 'It's a fine idea. I've heard you can get as much as ten pounds for a body that's fresh.

Think of the whisky we could buy with that?'

Burke felt the familiar pain begin in his groin. Now he was fully awake it wouldn't be long before the full force of the agony began once more. He knew there was only one thing that could push away that pain; whisky. 'Ten pounds you say?' he said to Hare, knowing he was already more than half committed to the idea.

'It's not like we're being resurrectionists.'

'No,' said Burke, genuinely shocked. 'Digging up a body from its eternal rest is certain damnation.'

'The man did die a natural death,' wheedled Hare.

'Has he no relatives?' asked Burke.

'None that will pay.'

Burke's fingers crept to his temples again as if he could massage his sluggish brain to life through his skull. 'So this would be a way of sorting out his estate and ensuring he entered the afterlife without debts on his soul?' he said thoughtfully. 'Do they bury the bodies when they're done with them? Do they get a decent Christian burial?'

Hare stood up bending and stretching out his knees. 'I'm sure they do, William. This is a civilised city.'

'Well, I suppose…'

This was good enough for Hare. 'I'll go get a barrel. We'll have to jam him in.'

Burke caught him by the wrist. 'Lord, no, Bill! We have to be more careful than that. It might not be a mortal crime we're planning, but it's still against the law of the city. The others will have talked. It'll be known we have a body in the house. We need to get the undertaker in.'

'We said no digging up the dead!'

'No, too risky anyway, even leaving the sinning aside. What we'll do is get a sack of waste bark from the tannery up the wynd. Then when the undertaker's about to screw the lid down I'll invite him back through for a dram – you do have a dram or two left, don't you Bill?'

Hare nodded in assent.

'Well then, while he and I are having a wee dram and

marking the time of day you'll be swapping the body for the sack and putting the lid back down.'

Hare thought for a moment. Burke waited for him to catch up. Hare scratched his chin and picked a flea out of his armpit. He cracked its back and flicked it to the floor. Finally he said, 'So he'll be screwing down a mess of bark all right and tight without him knowing it?'

'Exactly,' said Burke.

'That's a fine idea, William. One of the very best. You got one hell of a good education in Ireland. Why your brains are fit to bursting.'

'Do you know who we'll need to take him to?'

Hare touched the side of his nose. 'I know the people to ask. If you help me, William, I'll split the money with you.'

Much moved, Burke got to his feet despite the pain and offered his friend his hand. 'You always were the best of fellows!'

Hare grasped the smaller hand in his large grimy paw, the blackened fingers curled close to Burke's own white ones. Hare was never one for making the best of himself. Unlike Burke his ugliness would always overwhelm any attempt to smarten up, but Burke saw through it. He saw his friend as Hare said, 'Your back will never be cold while I'm around, my friend. We'll fight this life together.'

'So there you go,' said Burke snapping them back to his cold little cell. 'I couldn't rightly say which one of us had the idea. We sort of came up with it between us. And then when we did arrive at the good doctor's place, his man was very welcoming. Couldn't have treated us better if we'd been proper gentlemen. Indeed he kept saying how fresh bodies were always welcome and no questions asked.'

'And that tempted you?' said Rose. 'That one man opened up your path to the gallows?'

'Oh, I wouldn't be saying that,' said Burke reasonably. 'But it did make a mighty impression on us that this smart gentlemen in his fine, clean linen was offering us money as casual as if he were asking us to procure him a new pair of boots. It was no matter to him. Not worth the breaking of sweat when we heaved the corpse over his threshold.' Burke leaned towards Rose confidentially, 'We may not like them proper gents back in the Old Town, but we do respect them. And this was a doctor's man. A proper doctor the likes of me could never afford and he wasn't worried about his immortal soul. No, not one whit.' Burke sat back and turned his palms upward in an offering gesture. 'He was offering us money for something that weren't no use to its owner no more and what, he said, would advance the boundaries of medical science.'

'Much as you would care for that,' snapped back Rose.

'It's true that the only medicine many know in the Old Town is whisky. We're too poor to pay for a doctor. Why, I'd be surprised if even someone as well respected as yourself, Captain, could afford to pay for one of them to visit your family.'

Rose winced.

'And I say,' continued Burke watching him closely, 'that be no fair thing. The more doctors they train I reckon the less they will be able to charge. It won't be the high and mighty few it'll be a regular swarm of them. Think of that!'

'So you were doing a public service supplying the bodies?' sneered Rose.

'Oh well Captain, there's many a thing in life that is necessary but not palatable. Them young doctors need the bodies to train. You know most of them when they arrive wouldn't know what to do if a doxy lifted her skirts for free. Who wants a doctor who doesn't know their arse from their elbow? Could lead to some rare mistakes, that could!' Burke gave a throated chuckle. 'Sure, it does me a power of good talking to you, Captain. Quite takes my mind of my circumstances and my pain.'

But Rose was hardly listening. His vision swam red. 'So all your crimes were in the name of science?' he cried in disbelief.

Burke gave another chuckle. 'No, they were in the name of money, right enough.' Then he lent forward, suddenly serious. 'But that Dr Knox, he knew what we were doing. He didn't say a word and he don't take no blame. He was advancing science. I was making a living.'

The irony in Burke's voice was heavy, but Rose pushed it mentally aside. The knowledge that he couldn't afford a good doctor for Jenny was too painful. If he thought about it he would have to acknowledge that amongst all the viciousness, the greed and the murder, Burke was making some points that were all too valid. Instead he focussed on the man's greed. 'You made a fortune,' he accused.

Burke regarded him blankly for a moment. He seemed genuinely nonplussed at this turn of the conversation. 'Is that meant to stand against me?' he asked. When Rose gave him no answer he eventually continued. 'You know the Old Town, Captain. You know what it's become now the ones with the money have fled to their fancy houses in the New Town. Why I'll wager even you live in the Old Town. I'm sure it was a good civilised area where you were bringing up your family, but now even that is on its way down. It's a long time since you could pass a duke on the tenement stair. A long time since we all muddled on together. It's them and us now. And we're the ones left to rot.'

Rose sat with a stony face. He was determined not to let anything else show. Burke warmed to his theme. Internally Rose acknowledged he was a charismatic speaker; a diabolical speaker, mixing facts with his own warped perspective with a cunning ease.

'The conditions we live in,' continued Burke, 'the beggar's hostels with more families to a room than there are places to lay a head. No matter how the women clean there's the constant filth, the stench of piss and shit chucked into the street, the crying bairns running in rags half-starved, the fevers, the fetid air that spreads disease and the rats that run in hoards. It's wrong to ask anyone to live like this, wouldn't you say Captain? For you know the truth of it. The sheer persistent misery of it all. Don't you want to make that all go away? I know I do. I used to hold parties for the bairns when I was in funds. A little bit of happiness in their poor damned lives, damned before they were born. Can you look at them and not wish you could do something?'

Rose thought unwillingly of the toe-ragged boy.

Burke nodded. 'But we're only one man, aren't we Captain. You get tired. Tired of it all. That's what the whisky takes away. The misery of it all. Sure I'm weak for needing it. That's what I am. A man. Only a man. A man living like a dog. It's easy to lose sight of your humanity in the daily struggle to survive.'

'That's more likely the whisky,' snapped Rose.

Burke nodded. 'It does numb the pain in my crotch, so it does. This cancer's a nasty thing. You'd not believe what my balls look like now. Would you care to see?' Burke fumbled with the opening of his trousers.

'No, I would not!'

Burke did himself up again. 'Very wise, Captain. Horrible sight I tell you, horrible sight! The devil's sure got me by the balls!' He paused and cocked his head to one side. 'I don't suppose there's any chance of a wee dram, is there? Medicinal purposes like?'

'There's plenty that make an honest living,' said Rose. He could feel his sympathy slipping towards the ones who lived in the Old Town. Who lived that abject poverty and turned to crime only to try to make life bearable. That was almost understandable, he told himself, but what Burke had done, never. Never. He would never have sympathy for this man, this cunning devil who lied through his smiles. Who'd do anything, say anything, to get another sip of whisky.

Burke shook his head like a dog coming out of water. 'Eighteen months murdering and everyone forgets the thirty-five years I worked as an honest labourer and cobbler.' He paused, his head on one side, like a dog listening for his master's voice. 'Though I suppose I can see how they might put it out of their minds. The murdering being the more interesting part.'

'This no joke!' cried Rose, springing to his feet and sending the stool flying.

Burke also got to his feet, though he struggled slightly to rise. 'Is it not?' he said. 'Your criminal justice system is making a mockery of me. You know, everyone knows, I was far from being the only one involved in all this. At the very least you must acknowledge Hare was as guilty as me and he goes free. How is this right?' Burke took a step closer. 'Even in this gloom I can see it in your eyes, Captain. This situation puzzles you almost as much as I. We're educated men. At least I was well educated by the priests back in Ireland. Perhaps your education comes from the life you've led. But we are both reasoning beings and we know what is happening here is not right. I am called to pay the price for many.'

'You are a monster,' shouted Rose and pushed Burke roughly away from him. Burke fell awkwardly on one side, the breath winded out of him. He lay there, clutching his stomach, his face white and sweaty. Then he took several deep breaths and pulled himself up to a sitting position.

'You quite got me there, Captain. I never saw that coming and me a military man.'

Rose bent and picked up his stool. Now was his moment to leave, but he found himself setting the stool aright on the floor once more. 'You were a servant in the Donegal Militia,' he countered.

'Servant to an officer, Captain. My brother Constantine was a non-commissioned officer. And if I say so myself I was good at what I did and very well liked. Ah, it was a grand time I had serving my country.'

Burke paused. Rose felt himself invited to enter into fond reminisces of his army days. Images of bodies hacked, slashed, dead and dying, filled his mind's eye.

As if seeing into these thoughts Burke suddenly said, 'Why there's a thought! Why don't the army sell on the bodies of the dead? The enemy mind, so no one's offended. It would bring them a tidy income.' Burke rubbed his finger through the stubble on his right cheek. 'Though I daresay them doctors might complain they were too chopped up like. As if that weren't what they were going to do themselves! Probably try and beat the price so far down it would nae be worth the effort conveying them from the battlefield. Ah, well, if I have one idea I have thousands. Hare used to say my brains were fit to bursting. I reckon it's all about being able to see the world as it truly is and not how so many pretend it to be. Why, I remember…'

Rose cut off this ramble. 'How can you think such things?'

'Does your employ not teach you a practical turn of mind, Captain? Soldiering in any form breeds a familiarity with death.'

'There are degrees of familiarity,' said Rose coldly.

Burke slapped his hands on his thighs. 'Why almost a joke! We'll be friends yet, I tell you. But think Captain, when you've been as poor as I then it changes the way you look at the world. You have the luxury of being a by the book man.'

'That is my duty. To uphold the law…'

'And root out such chaotic elements as myself. I know that Captain. Listen now, I'll tell you a difference between us. I have the sense that it will help you. If needs be you'd put your kin in here, would you not?'

Rose blinked at the sudden question. 'If they broke the law,' he said.

'You'd not turn a blind eye if you could?'

'No. That way everything unravels,' said Rose. 'For laws to work they have to apply to all equally.'

Burke grinned. Then he peered closer at Rose in the poor light and his smile faded. 'Why I do believe you believe that,' he said. 'I don't think I'll waste our time with a long argument about how the laws do not and will never be applied equally to all, because I can see you are a serious fellow – you tries to do just that.' He shook his head. 'It must make your life very hard.'

Rose began to protest, but Burke cut him off. 'The

difference between us is that I'd move heaven and earth to keep those I loved out of such a place as this.'

Rose shifted uncomfortably. 'You're twisting my words.'

'Not at all,' replied Burke calmly. 'Hare and our two women were all I cared about in this world. I took no delight in the murdering. I've heard some men get into the enjoyment of killing, but not I. But the truth is, it caused me no pain either. Everyone outside our little band was – well outside. Not one of us. They were hardly real.'

'That's a terrible way to think.'

'Ah Captain, if you but knew it's the way that most folk think. They just do not admit it – even to themselves.'

Rose floundered. Thoughts collided in his head, but all he could come up with was, 'There's plenty poor who don't turn their hand to murdering.'

'Then they've had more luck than me,' said Burke, shaking his head. 'They disbanded the Militia. Got rid of us. And I had to give up my fine uniform.' He looked forlornly down at his torn and dirtied coat and shirt. With his fingers he traced the outline of his beloved uniform. 'It suited me that. I cut quite a figure.' Then he shot Rose a blinding grin. 'Not that you're so bad yourself Captain, but these Scotch uniforms they don't have quite the style of the Irish. Which brings me round to my old point. When you saw Hare did he send any message to me? Only I'm wondering has he mentioned my money?'

'What?' asked Rose.

'I'm owed on that last body.'

It took a moment for Burke's comments to register with Rose. Then without a word he picked up his stool and left. Burke's voice followed him. 'What did I say? Like the young doctor said, it was only a business transaction. Don't you want to hear the rest of my story?'

Rose didn't see Burke let out a sigh of relief or his face collapse into pain as he curled himself into a ball and wrapped his arms around himself.

IV

That night as Rose left the guardhouse he knew he was being watched. The guards on duty at the fire pit nodded curtly to him. The tall lanky lad with acne and hair long enough he knew he should comment on it, and the fat old-timer who most often got left at the gaol as he could no longer run, but was as swift with a boot or a fist as his younger compatriots when a prisoner got out of line, would normally have given him some evening greeting. Tonight it was only a nod; their eyes not quite meeting his. The truth of it felt cold in his stomach. They're talking about me, he thought. Everyone is wondering why I spend so much time with that monster. The truth of it was he no longer knew himself. He made a resolution then to not return. The last time he would see Burke would be when he mounted the gallows he told himself.

He walked along the Royal Mile. A link bearer ran past him, smoke guttering from his torch. The bangs and crashes coming from St Giles told him the stalls were closing shop for the night. Here and there candles glimmered in the windows of tenement houses. It wouldn't be long before all uncovered fire sources would have to be extinguished. Fire remained the terror of the Old Town. High above him a woman comforted a crying child. They were five storeys high into the night sky. Should a fire start below them they would never escape.

He brushed shoulders with a number of people on the way home. Most tried to give him a wide enough berth as a courtesy to his uniform, but there was a hurry to be off the streets, to be home and sorted for the night. It would not be long before the wild dogs and those whose business flourished better under darkness would be about. All around him as he went down echoed the clangs of the closes as people locked the metal gates that separated the entryway into their tenement courtyards from the wider, wilder Royal Mile.

Rose arrived home to a clean house and quiet children. All was much as it had been the night before. Sarah's smile of greeting was a little more fixed and even in the fading light he could see her eyes were red from crying. His two little boys launched themselves at him the moment he was through the door and clung tight.

'Is Jenny no better?' he asked his wife.

'She sleeps,' said Sarah. 'I'm sure the rest is doing her good.' She bustled over to the table. 'I got you a fine meal for your supper and a bottle of best ale.'

'Such a feast,' said Rose, sitting down at the table and depositing the two children into their chairs. 'Now would there be anyone who'd like a slice of my pie?'

Two little faces lit up. 'Me! Me!'

'You'd think I spent my day starving the wee things,' complained Sarah half-heartedly. 'Don't give too much away, Hugh. You work hard and need your food.'

'Who could resist faces like this,' said Rose as he slipped a slice in front of each of his sons.

'You spoil them,' said Sarah, but her tone was gentle.

'I wish I could,' said Rose. 'I wish I could.' He took a deep breath. 'When you were growing up Sarah how bad was it?'

A shadow passed over his wife's face and she turned away. 'Bad enough.'

'Did you ever have to…' Rose's mouth fought clumsily for the right words. 'Did you ever have to do things that…that…'

'Why are you asking this now?' Sarah got up from the table and began to tidy away the boys' toys.

'It's not that I'm for casting up any blame, love,' said Rose.

'Lately, I've come to question what drives men to do what they do – or women for that matter. I see poverty around me every day, but I've never been a part of it.'

Sarah still had her back to him. 'I don't want to talk about this Hugh. We've got Jenny sick and that's enough worry for me.'

Rose stood up and went over to her. He placed his hands on her shoulders. 'I wasn't meaning to upset you, love,' he said softly. Sarah reached up to place her hand on top of one of his. She turned towards him and he saw tears running down her face.

'I wouldn't wish the grinding poverty we have in this city on my worst enemy,' she said. 'There's a point, a line you cross when you stop being human. You're an animal intent on survival. Nothing more.' They were speaking in whispers now so the children would not hear.

Rose stroked her hair. 'Was it that bad for you?'

'You rescued me,' said Sarah. 'It was a lifetime ago. Another life. I've no mind to revisit it.'

And with that Rose had to be content. Over the years, during the long nights of caring and feeding their young children they had talked of many things. Rose had shared his thoughts and what little education he had with his new wife and she had proved a quick study. She had a lively mind and enjoyed their debates, but tonight it seemed he had come too near the bone. She had never told him how she was living before they met, but Rose had his suspicions. He wished she would tell him, so he could tell her that he didn't care, that he loved her despite the depths to which fate had led her. Even after all these years he sensed she clung to her secrets, terrified that knowing the truth would belittle her in his eyes. But it wouldn't. She was his helpmate, the mother of his children and the other part of his soul. He would forgive her anything that was past. It was time such things were spoken of.

'I wouldn't care, you know, Sarah. Whatever you had to do. It would make no difference to the love and respect I have for you.'

His wife gave a low gasp of astonishment and her hand went up to his face, cupping his cheek. Her eyes were wide with wonder.

'I wouldn't care, Sarah,' he said fiercely. 'You are my wife and mother to my children. Whatever you've had to do I know you are a good woman. I…'

Any other words were lost as Sarah pressed her mouth to his and kissed him passionately.

'Ugh,' came the chorus from the two little boys at the table.

'Disgusting,' said Jamie.

V

The rain fell in stair rods on Rose's head as he walked to work through the early morning light. But the Captain of the Guard walked with a light step. Last night they had moved Jenny, still sleeping, back to her own bed. Then he and Sarah had warmed their own bed in the way that is expected of married couples. Yet, it had been different. Sarah had been as keen and passionate as when they had first met. It was as if his comments to her had removed something that lay between them and they were meeting for the first time again as new and untried lovers.

'I didnae know wha tae do,' said the sergeant mournfully. 'It's no like I can refuse a priest. Maybe if yer were ta hav a wee word with him. The others they're saying yer oft speaking wi' him.' The man picked his nose with a blackened and broken fingernail as he waited for Rose's answer. He inspected his slimy yellow and green treasure as if he had never seen the like. He had been on all night and, never the cleanest of men, this morning he was rank with stale sweat. There must have been some disturbance last night. A purple bruise blossomed through his patchy white beard on his jaw but there was no comment about this, only complaints about the priest. 'I didnae ken how they'd all fit.'

Rose's mood sunk to his boots. 'I'll have a word with him,' he said and turned to leave before the sergeant could consume his prize.

As he descended down the darkened stairway the cries of the prisoners around him were unusually loud. One woman was wailing as if her lungs would burst. On his way, Rose found one of the guards and curtly demanded he 'see to that female'. It was only after he had passed on that he had pause to think how the guard might interpret his order. He had made it known throughout the gaol that he did not condone the beating or abusing of the women housed there, but there was a mood in the air, and an atmosphere that he couldn't quite put his finger on. All the men were jumpy, as if waiting for the shadows to attack, and the prisoners were restless. Even those he thought had long given up to despair moaned and muttered at him as he made his way down. But he did not do immediately what the guard had asked. First he went to see Hare. There was no side to this miserable man. He didn't beguile with his words. He was a cold-blooded murderer. Hare was the reality of what they had done. Burke was the illusion.

He flung open the cell door and demanded. 'I want to hear about the murders.' He had barely uttered the words when a fit of coughing overcame him. This cell was beyond foul. The slop bucket had become a slop corner. It was clear that Hare still suffered from the prison food and that no one was clearing out his cell in any way.

Hare was lying curled in a ball; a picture of misery. He raised his head slightly from the grimy floor, 'All of them?'

'Yes,' said Rose.

Hare pushed himself up to a half-sitting position. He squinted against the harsh light of Rose's lantern. 'That would be a long story, Your Honour. It's all been told in the courtroom. My telling it again won't bring anyone back.'

Rose strode across the cell. The floor squelched under his feet. 'Sixteen men and women. One young lad. How can you live with what you've done?'

Hare pushed one hand through his greasy locks, moving the hair away from his face. He frowned. 'I reckoned if William could cope, him being the more religious-like, so could I.'

Rose turned sharply and spat, 'Didn't you realise it was

wrong, man?'

Hare cringed. He curled down into a ball once more. His eyes were startling white against his dirt-streaked face. 'I don't understand, Your Honour,' he pleaded. 'William's an educated man. He explained it all to me. How we had to do it.'

Rose spat on the floor. He turned on his heel and made for the door.

'Do I have your leave to go yet, Your Honour?' came Hare's voice behind him. It sounded thin and wheedling. 'It's mighty cold and damp down here. Is not your business with me finished?'

Rose pushed his shoulders back and stretched out his neck, hearing it click. He felt armoured. He had seen the truth; now he could face Burke.

'Good to see you again, Captain,' came the cheery cry from the gloom. Rose's skin prickled. He had a sudden sense that all that was wrong in this place was due to housing Burke, the monster Burk e. As he looked into the smiling face in front of him, thick with grime, but still undeniably one of the better-looking men in the gaol, with all his hair and a full set of teeth, he willed himself to remember this man was a monster. He had killed more men and women than any man Rose had ever come across. More than anyone had ever come across. This wasn't like his Sarah doing whatever she had, to keep body and soul together as a child and young woman, this was an adult male with a good trade at his fingertips, who had no reason to cross the line into depravity. Whatever the trappings, this man was no better than Hare.

'Yer looking perplexed, Captain. Did you not have a good night? I've got a funny story to tell you myself. I was dreaming I was back with my Nell we were engaging in what any good man and wife do of a dark evening, when Nell started kissing my ear. It was alright at first. An odd thing for her to do, but not unpleasant. But it got so it was so ticklish it was distracting. That was when I woke up and bless me if there wasn't this big beastie with six lang dangling legs shuggling about in me lug. Took me nigh on ten minutes I shouldn't wonder to get the creature out. And there was I thinking Nell was whispering sweet nothings in my ears.' Burke laughed loudly at his story. His laughter faded when he didn't even win a smile from Rose. 'Sure, how is my Nell?'

'Locked up for her own protection,' said Rose shortly.

'Ah, me poor Nell. What will become of her now without her protector?'

'That wailing you can hear. That's her.'

'No,' said Burke, appearing genuinely shocked. 'Poor, poor Nell.'

Rose drew up his stool. 'You profess to love this woman?'

'Aye,' said Burke.

'And yet there are multiple accounts of you beating her.'

'Sure, she was my wife. It's not a crime for a man to beat his own wife if she's needing it. Do you not beat yours, Captain?'

'No.'

'What never? Still, I'm sure you married a genteel woman. Women like my Nell have to be kept in check. It was my job to school her, wild, uneducated creature that she was.'

'And to let Hare beat her too?'

'We were close. Like family.'

'Did she have any part in the murders?'

'Nay,' said Burke, shifting to a more comfortable position on the floor. 'If she was smarter she might have kent what we were about, but we always sent the women away. Her only part was drinking the profits. And that she did well and gladly.'

Rose sat back and stretched out his legs. 'The guards tell me you've had four priests in here today and that they are all to attend your hanging. It's going to be mighty crowded up there.'

'Sure, if it's too crowded I'll happily give up my place to any of them.'

'Would you? My wife told me last night that the papers are

reporting you'd not accept a pardon even if you were offered one.'

'So she can read. I was sure she'd be a genteel lady.'

'Is it true?'

'I don't think I'm likely to be called to test the veracity of that statement, do you Captain?' Burke's eyes crinkled into laughter lines. 'But I've made my confession.'

'Several times and all with differences.'

'It's funny you should say that Captain. I've been thinking. I have a lot of time now for thinking. Especially as I have no whisky to calm my brain. Time seems to stretch in the dark, but every morning comes too quickly for it brings me closer to my maker and the sooner to exit God's green earth.' Burke heaved a huge sigh.

'You should have been on the stage,' said Rose.

'You think? I would have fetched a fine figure that's for sure and I tell me tales well. Which brings me back to those confessions. I found myself midway through telling the stories when I started to wonder if I did do what Hare alleged I'd done. I used to drink so much whisky to dull the pain that my facilities were fair pickled most of the time. You know how it is with a good tale, you get into your way of telling it, you know the rhythm, the pace of it, when to make your listener laugh, when to make them cry and it's like the story takes you over. You say what you must to make up a good tale. Cos you see when I listen to myself describing what I've done I can't believe it. I can't believe that Mr and Mrs Burke's wee boy could ever have done such things. The lad that loved the countryside and learning his scripture. The good cobbler everyone trusted. How could he have done all these things? Sure, it's like a nightmare, it is.'

The silence lay heavy between them. Rose felt deep within him if he answered this speech, if he gave it any credence, then he would be on the slippery path to sympathising with this monster. He understood that the man lying before him on the ground was as cunning a creature as he had ever met.

'I visited Hare again,' he said, thinking to unsettle Burke.

But Burke only gave another of his grins. 'How fares my old comrade?'

'He's eager to be released.'

Burke made a short snorting noise.

'You still resent him?' asked Rose, pushing his point.

'We'll meet again,' said Burke in a low voice. 'In Hell.'

'He says it was all your scheming.'

'I never set a hair outside the law till I met him. Hah! Wait! I never set a hair outside the law till I met Hare. That's clever that. My brain is working without me even knowing it!'

'And yet Hare says he was the upright citizen till he met you.'

'Then one of us is lying.'

Rose put his fingers to his temples and massaged them. 'You've told over and over again how the first sale was mere chance. How did you go on from there?'

'And again I bring out the student of human nature in you, Captain. Well, I suppose it went something like this. Listen.'

Ice cracked under Burke's boots as he made his way across the small lodging to where Hare was beckoning him. His friend's dark complexion was made the worse for the ferocious frown on his face. Burke clapped him on the back. 'That was a fine drop of whisky we had last night and no mistake. Morning's always the worst, hey my friend.'

'Come away into the passage, William. There's something we need to discuss.'

Burke glanced across at the Gray family who were stretching and waking, knowing their time upon the mattresses was almost up until tonight. The wife was poking among the straw for the two children's stockings. They were forever losing them. Though how they could bare to sleep without them Burke had no idea. Hare pushed open the door to the passage and even colder air blew in. By instinct the Grays huddled closer. To Burke it felt like a hard slap in the face, but the air was fresh, making him realise how frowsy the room had become. Only the old soldier in the corner did not stir.

Burke pulled the door to behind him before the children could start to wail. 'So what is it you're not wanting the Grays to hear?'

Hare pulled out a much-abused cap from his pocket and plonked it on his head, pulling it as far down as he could as if it might also mask his face as well as insulate his head. Burke blew on his fingers, waiting for his old friend to speak. The passageway was bare. Not even the rats were venturing from their holes today.

'It's the old man in the corner,' said Hare at last.

'The Sassenach?'

'Aye him. He's had the fever.'

'Dear God, Bill, you've got to tell the Grays. They have children.'

Hare put his hand on Burke's shoulder to hold him in place. 'There, now that's why I didn't tell you. I knew you with your do-gooding ways would be right off to warn them and I cannae afford to lose the business.'

'My Nelly. Her bairn,' gasped Burke. 'You've put them both at risk.'

'What's done is done, William. I'll admit it was a risk, but it was a choice between warning them and losing our home. Sleeping rough in this weather would guarantee a fever. You've got to admit that.'

'Aye, well, there's something in that,' said Burke reluctantly. 'But at least you're telling me now.'

Hare winced. 'I said he had the fever.'

There was a long pause between them, then Burke spoke, 'You mean he's…he's…'

'No, not quite, but I reckon he's on his way out.'

'What's the thinking, Bill?' Burke asked, suspicion clouding his eyes.

The outer door opened, blasting them with yet colder air, and a woman staggered in carrying a basket of washing almost equal to her own size. She was no more than twenty-four years old, but already she had lost most of her teeth and while her blonde hair retained an impression of the beauty she must once have been, her skin was pockmarked and raddled with the past effects of cheap drink. 'Morning to you, mother,' said Hare doffing his cap to her. She ignored him, but returned Burke's cheery salute with a slight smile. Both men waited while she began to make her ponderous way up the stairs huffing and puffing. By the time Burke was sure she was gone, both he and Hare were stamping their feet and almost doing an impromptu jig in an effort to get warm.

'Jesus, Mary and Joesph, I thought she'd never get up them stairs.'

'You could have offered to help her,' said Burke.

'I'm not in the habit of helping hags with their loads and I didn't want to be giving her any reason to remember today.'

'Bill,' said Burke, 'what is it you're thinking?'

Hare lent in even closer. 'I've been told that it's in the last stages that the fever is all the more catching.'

'No,' said Burke, alarmed. Then his eyes narrowed. 'Who told you this? It wouldn't have anything to do with young Patterson would it?'

Hare punched him playfully on the arm. 'There you go,' he said encouragingly, 'I knew you'd be quick to catch on.'

'You're suggesting murder,' said Burke.

'Hush. Hush,' said Hare. 'The old man's more than half over death's threshold. For all I know he's breathed his last while we were standing freezing our balls off out here.'

'Which would be mighty convenient.'

'Don't be sassy, Bill. You'll not deny the money would come in handy? New coat? Another bottle or two of whisky?'

'I'm not denying I wouldn't be liking having either or both, but murder, Bill?'

'We'd be putting the poor old sod out of his suffering, so we would,' said Hare. 'If I was him, wheezing and gasping my last, I'd be right glad if some kind man put me out of my misery.'

'Would you?' asked Burke.

'Aye, I would. I mean it William. If I catch the fever from that Sassenach, like that I want you, as my best friend, to put me out of my misery. Promise me that at least? I'm mortal feart of feeling those last breaths. The agony of my ribs squeezing the life out of my lungs. Knowing there's nothing I can do, but lie there helpless, in pain, waiting for the Angel of Death to come take me.'

Burke shivered. 'It's a bad way to go that's for sure. You've quite a way with words Bill Hare. I'll have nightmares for weeks.'

'No, you won't,' said Hare. 'If you follow my plan you'll be having the sweet dreams that only the whisky can bring.'

'But murder…'

'Ah, give over William. You're like a nagging wife. You know what I'm saying is right. And I'm telling you we can have our whisky and that poor old man can have his peace and no-one be any the wiser. Why, I even know how to do it, so we don't cause the old fellow any more pain.'

'No pain?'

'No pain and more whisky.'

'I wish to God we had some now,' said Burke.

'We'll be having it soon enough, William. Now take a wee shifty round the door. Are the Grays ready to leave yet?'

Burke put his eye to the crack between the door and the wall. 'She's found the last pair of stockings. I can see the wee one's feet.'

Hare grabbed him by the collar. 'Come on then. The last thing we need is for them to find us standing out here with that expression on your face.'

'What expression?' protested Burke, but he followed his friend out.

'Like you're a dog that's going to be hanged tomorrow. Come on now. I'll buy you a wee dram to give you heart. One mind.'

'And explain to me how we're going to do it?'

'Not in a public place William,' said Hare shaking his head. 'And you the bright one.'

Within the hour they were winding their way back up towards Hare's lodging. Their path's erratic nature due not to inebriation, Hare's coin had indeed not stretched beyond one drink a piece, but because they had taken care in the bar to sit with a group of fishermen, who escaping their wives were happily reliving the adventures of the night's fishing. Before they left the group had passed out and Burke and Hare intended to be back among them when they awoke. 'As if we had never left,' said Hare. He grabbed Burke by the collar and pulled him into an alley. 'Have you no got eyes in your head this morning, William-boy? That's that damn washerwoman, Mrs Ostler.'

Burke peeled Hare's fingers off his coat. 'It's not that fine, Bill. But it's the best I got.'

'Do you want to swing in it?' asked Hare in a whisper, gravelly with anger.

'And there was me thinking you were trying to talk me into this enterprise,' said Burke.

'Whisky, William, whisky.'

'I'm just saying you're not being that encouraging.'

'That'll be because I don't have your way with words. Now shut your yap, we're here.'

Hare opened the door to his rooms tentatively. The shutters were open no more than a crack with one pale slice of morning light cutting across the room. Burke squeezed in behind Hare. Both of them holding their breath and walking as lightly as they could. The old man gave a rattling wheeze from his bed by the far wall.

'Maybe he's croaked,' whispered Burke very softly in Hare's ear. Hare put his hand back to hold Burke in place. They waited together in the semi-darkness. As his eyes adjusted Burke could see clearly that the rest of the room's occupants had left. He had no clear memory of where Nell had said she'd be off to this morning. He wondered if she had left him again and he hadn't noticed. The old man wheezed again suddenly; the noise sharp as a whip-crack to Burke and Hare, who both staggered back in surprise. Hare stood heavily on Burke's feet, but Burke didn't even squeak.

'Looks like we've a job to do after all,' said Hare softly.

'Could we no wait until he passes?' asked Burke. 'It sounds as if he's close.'

'Every moment we wait is one moment more when we could be catching the fever.'

'Or our wives coming back,' muttered Burke under his breath.

Hare began to roll up his shirt sleeves. 'Let's be at it,' he said. 'What you need to do it pinch his nose and put your hand over his mouth, so no breath or sound can escape him. I'll lay on him, so he can't twist under your grip.'

'Wouldn't it be better for you to be at the business end, so to speak? Seeing as you know how it's to be done?'

'No, William. All them years cobbling, pushing that needle through that hard leather has given you a strength in your fingers the like of which is hard to better.'

'How long will I need to hold him Bill?'

'Until he's dead,' said Hare, exasperated.

'But how long with that be?'

'How should I know? It's not like I've done this before. Now, have at it. The sooner we begin the sooner it's over.'

Hare strode quickly across the room and stood by the old man's bed. Burke followed him hesitantly. He stopped a pace from the bed. Hare raised his eyebrows, a gesture which was totally lost in the gloom. Burke stayed where he was. Hare gestured furiously until Burke took up his position at the head of the bed. 'Like this,' he mouthed and made a motion with his hands to show what Burke was to do. Burke couldn't see too clearly. He certainly couldn't lip-read, but he understood all too well what Hare meant. He looked down at the sleeping man. His hair was wild and tangled. Dirt had sunk deep into the crags of his face. He brought his face down and saw a silver trickle of saliva running away from the old man's mouth. His forehead sparkled with sweat and he smelled, oh how he smelled of old onions, piss and shit. Burke fought back bile as his body heaved. You got inured to the foul smells of the Old Town, but the man smelled far worse. He smelled, Burke thought, like death. Hare was signalling to him again, growing more and more frantic. Burke didn't want to put his naked hand over that mouth. Next time I'll wear gloves he thought and then immediately corrected himself. There would be no next time. He was doing this old man a favour, putting him out of his misery. That he would get whisky out of it was but a pleasurable side effect.

He nodded curtly to Hare and lunged forward. He felt the gristle of the man's nose as he pinched the nostrils. As his hand pushed down on the mouth he felt the lips shift against the remaining teeth. The whisky seemed to vanish from his system and he was all at once sober and horribly aware of what he was doing. He threw his whole weight behind it so the man might not twist and fight. He found he was as terrified at the thought of the man waking as he was of killing him. Hare took the signal and threw himself across the legs.

The old man's eyes flew open. Faint blue, with red streaks through the yellowish white, they bored into Burke's. He let his grip weaken for a moment. The old man's eyes darted back and forwards frantically and he twisted weakly beneath Burke's hands. Like an animal trying to escape, thought Burke.

'Fuck man,' cried Hare, pushing down the bucking legs. 'Get it over with it!'

Burke turned his head away and crushed the nose beneath his hands. A crunch and click told him the nose had broken. The old man gave a muffled cry. Burke held on. The man's cries became more frequent, but weaker. 'Sorry,' muttered Burke. 'Nothing personal, old man.' He looked back down at the face and saw the eyes begin to lose focus. He was almost gone. He pressed down all the further and heard Hare cry out.

'The bugger's pissed on me!'

The old man's back arched. There was a final shudder and he was gone.

Burke stood back and leaned against the damp wall. 'All for the sake of whisky,' he said.

Hare lashed out at the body. 'Look at me,' he said angrily, 'I'm covered in piss!' Burke slid weakly down the wall. He watched Hare rage and laughter welled up inside him. A moment later they were both laughing with relief. Burke was surprised to find tears streaming down his face.

'Old age is a cruel affliction and crueller yet when it comes with poverty,' said Burke.

Captain Rose snorted. 'So you were most affected by the old man's troubles and were doing him a favour. Killing him gave you no pleasure?'

'Aye, it did not,' said Burke, raising his voice for the first time in their exchange 'I cut short his suffering as the noose is like to do for mine.'

'You refer to your cancer?' said Rose.

'Another blessing from the good Lord. This time right in the balls.'

'That's blasphemy!' exclaimed Rose.

Burke sat back and lowered his voice. 'God and I have a complicated relationship. I am his creature and only capable of what he allowed me to be. It's all a question of the conflict between predestination and free will.'

'We'll have none of our Papist claptrap here,' said Rose, his voice like a whip.

'That's not particularly Papist, Captain.' He paused and leaned in once more, his eyes seeking contact with Rose's. 'Are you a man who knows his scripture? I know the good book very well. I could recommend a few good passages if you like. If I hadn't been burned out of my home that time I'd be able to lend you some interesting tracts.' He sighed. 'Another blessing of the Lord. Nell and I bare escaped with our lives.'

'Fire is not uncommon in Edinburgh.' said Rose dismissively. 'Especially among drunkards.'

'I see you are a man who reduces everything to its simplest solution,' said Burke. 'There's much to be said for that point of view. It gives life a clarity. Though to my mind it's missing many of the intricacies of living.'

'How dare you try to debate with me like a reasoning man!' shouted Rose. 'You are nothing but a monster.'

'Hey! Hey!' said Burke, holding up his hands in surrender. 'What did I say?'

But Rose was up and stalking to the door, his stool dragging behind him. 'I will stay and listen to no more of this.'

'I'll look forward to your next visit, Captain,' called Burke. 'Don't be a stranger. I'm not here for much longer.'

VI

'It was like a dog had got up on its hind legs and started talking,' complained Rose to his wife.

'Hmm,' said Sarah, wiping Jamie's chin.

'I mean he talks to me about the cruelty of poverty and how God forsakes a man in misery. How some lives are naught but suffering. As if he were doing the kindly thing by extinguishing them! I…'

'Oh Hugh, I've heard more than enough about this Burke,' snapped Sarah. 'Your only daughter lies next door barely able to speak and all you can do is moan at me about how this monster bends your ear. Stop visiting him. Walk away. It's not long now before he hangs. You're like a man possessed.'

'Barely,' said Rose. 'You mean Jenny is speaking again?'

Sarah gave an enormous sigh. 'No, not really. I didn't mean to say anything to you yet. It's early days.'

'What does the hag upstairs say?'

Sarah looked away past her husband into the far distance. 'Nothing good,' she said softly. 'Mary is not for giving us much hope.'

'She thinks Jenny is going to die?'

Jamie and Ben burst into tears at this. Sarah hushed them and sent furious glances at her husband. 'No, no, my little loves. She isn't going to die. Why don't you get down from the table and go and play in the corner before bedtime. She lowered her voice and hissed at Rose, 'She's convinced the fever has robbed Jenny of her wits.'

Rose stared at her, blinking back tears. 'No. You said it was early days yet.'

'She understands me,' said Sarah. 'She can do as I ask, but she tires easily. I reckon she will be abed for some time yet. Her speech is mostly gone. With the Lord's help I pray it will return.'

'But what will become of her?' blurted Burke.

'For heaven's sake, Hugh, be quiet. You'll upset the children again. It's in the Lord's hands now.'

'But you know as well as I, Sarah, anyone who appears lacking in wits – and lack of speech is often seen to be the same even if it is not true – anyone looking witless cannot get work, cannot earn a living. She'll end up wandering the streets and…'

'We will look after her,' said Sarah with finality.

'But we cannot live forever.'

'Then if the worst should come we must ask one of her brothers to look after her.'

'It's hard enough to earn a living for yourself and the two of them will have their own families one day.'

'Then we will have to pray the good Lord takes her early,' said Sarah bitterly. Rose started back in shock. 'What else do you expect me to say?' continued his wife. 'Yes, I know what a hard life she could have and there's things that will happen to her without our protection that I cannot bear to think of.'

Rose reached across the table and took his wife's hand. 'We will pray,' he said. 'We will pray she yet recovers and Mary is wrong.'

Sarah nodded and began to clear the table. Conversation for the rest of the evening was forced between them and Rose spent much of his time playing soldiers with his sons on the floor.

The next morning the grey sky grizzled over Edinburgh. Rose shrugged himself further into his coat, turning up his collar. He preferred the onslaught of rain they had had the day before to this fine, fine spray from the heavens. This type of weather led to you suddenly finding yourself wet through without ever fully realising it was raining. It was a cold, chilly nothing that seeped into your bones. It was also not enough to keep the people off the street. Instead merchants hurried past him, their heads well down and their pockets all the more ripe for picking due to their inattention. Equally the cold would drive more of the poor to rob; money needed for kindling and food. The cold increased appetites tenfold. When the sun shone, and Rose admitted that seemed rarer and rarer these days, people were more likely to make do or so the number admitted to his gaol told him. But these dark, grey days of misery made those living on the edge more likely to tip into crime.

Rose spied the boy in the toe-rags again. He was hovering around the stalls of St Giles. As he watched, the boy waylaid a passerby and started talking and pointing. With surprise, Rose realised he was hawking for a stallholder. Someone had given him a chance and the boy was going to make the most of it. The man he had stopped, all wrapped up his cloak and floppy hat, was drawn slowly and without mercy towards the stall. By the time Rose drew level he was counting out pennies and buying some candles that he had doubtless no intention of buying when he left his home, but would use none the less. Rose winked at the boy, who ducked his head and scuttled back to the street to find his next victim.

Rose moved on down the street, the walk so familiar to him he could do it blindfolded. The stones of the Old Town had once been as golden as their fresh New Town cousins. Today, even with the surfaces slick with rain they remained an unforgiving grey and the rain fell off the walls like never-ending tears. It was a day to count your miseries.

'Going to see him again, are you…Sir?' Rose picked up on the pause and gave the man a hard look. He was a lanky one, barely the other side of twenty and his face sprouted two boils on the point of popping. When he opened his mouth, Rose could see his central teeth were missing and tell he had a fondness for cheap meat pies.

'It's part of my duty, Sergeant, to ensure the monster does not destroy himself before his execution.'

The sergeant bowed his head. He was a young man and he was newly promoted. Rose recalled he had a wife and a new baby. 'How's your little girl?' he asked.

The sergeant shrugged. 'Not been right since she was born. Tiny, mewling thing. I think the good Lord will be calling her soon enough. Wife's very upset, of course, but it's the way of nature.' He shrugged again.

'I'm sorry,' said Rose. 'If you need to shorten your shifts…'

'No,' cut in the young man quickly. 'There's no need, Sir. Her mother's with her and I'd – I'd rather keep busy. Doctor says there's no reason why she shouldn't have more bairns.'

Rose, not knowing what to say, nodded briefly and made his way to his office. He was behind reading reports, which was saying something as few of his staff could write. He fussed over shifts, over the need for new men, and he called men in for verbal reports on the latest admissions and details of how the incarcerated were faring. His stomach was growling for lunch long before he was finished and he realised how much he had been neglecting his duties.

Rose held out for most of the day. He was on the point of calling it a day when it occurred to him that it honestly was his duty to check on Burke. He was the most notorious prisoner in the gaol and most closely his responsibility. Accordingly he made his way towards his cell. He was relieved to see the lanky sergeant was no longer on duty.

Burke blinked furiously in the light of Rose's lantern. 'Sure, I didnae think you were coming to see me today,' he said, raising a hand to shield himself against the light. 'I'm most glad to see you. No soul has been near me this day and it gets a mite lonely down here for a man as gregarious as myself. I don't know who's on shift, but I had my bread thrust through the door like it was a missile intended to do me harm. Sure they crusts are hard enough to do one a deal of damage if they hit you in the wrong place.'

Rose pulled up his stool and sat down. 'So you've not killed yourself today.'

'And I have no intention of so doing, Captain. I told you that's a mortal sin.'

'And you are a good Christian.'

'This is old ground, Captain. I know why you're here. You want to hear more about what happened with the shots.'

'Shots?'

'That's what we called our victims when we had one in the house. Kind of shorthand Hare and I worked up between us.'

Rose sagged against the wall. Almost at once he could feel the sour dampness seeping into his back but, not intending to stay, he had not brought his stool with him this time.

'Yer don't wanting to be doing that, Captain,' warned Burke. 'It'll take yer fine wife a long time to purge this stinking smell from yer uniform. Sure, I don't smell it that bad myself having being in here so long. It's amazing what you can get used to, isn't it? Why when I first got put in here I heaved up my guts, so I did. It was amazing to my mind that something could smell worse than the Old Town, but I have to give your guards credit, they have created a truly vile place to lodge such as I have never known. And for the most part, as I've said, they're not that bad a lot. Why, I've had some fine conversations with some of them once we got the introductory beatings over with. Not as good as you and I, of course, but then for the most part they aren't men of great learning are they? But then life itself can be a great teacher and I've managed to interest a couple of them in the more philosophical aspects of life…Captain? Do you heed me?'

Rose could feel his knees beginning to buckle. He wedged himself more tightly against the wall. He was no more religious than the next man, but he felt a wave of despair wash over him. How could God allow such evil in the world? Such evil and such hardship.

'Ah, now Captain, I think you need to be sitting down. Why don't you call for another of your men to bring you your seat? I don't like the look of your face. Even in this half-light I can see you've gone as white as the dead. Do you feel unwell? Or is something upsetting you?'

Rose blinked. 'You affect concern for me?'

'Sure, I do,' said Burke easily. 'We're friends, are we not? Or as like as friends as I am like to have!' He chuckled at his own joke. Then his face grew serious. 'And you've treated me well. Made this incarceration less of a torment with our conversations. I can tell you're a good man. Life hasn't sent you down any wrong paths. I wish you nothing but the best.'

'Shots,' croaked Rose.

'Was it that that upset you?' asked Burke. 'I could hardly go around speaking about how I'd found another victim for the doctors, could I? But I'm guessing you're thinking it was a mite unfeeling to talk of another human being in such a way?'

Rose rubbed his hand over his eyes.

'Hi!' called Burke. 'Yer Captain needs his seat! C'mon on Jamie, I ken it's you on duty. Stop stuffing yer face with the best bits of my dinner and bring your man his stool.'

Rose's mind was crowded with images of his daughter, the lanky guard's dying baby and the young boy in toe-rags. All of them so young to deal with the fates they had been dealt. Sleep, he told himself, I need sleep. I need to get out of this cell and go home and sleep. He barely noticed when Jamie opened the door and handed him the stool. He took it automatically and set it against the wall, so he could continue to lean there. Burke's face swam into his vision. What appeared to be genuine concern contorted his features. Rose made a grab for him, but he whatever was over taking him was also making him clumsy. Burke danced easily out of reach. 'There,' Burke said, 'I knew a seat would improve you.'

Words formed deep within him and rose without his volition. 'You're a monster.'

'Ah Captain,' said Burke. 'I am disappointed. I thought we had gone beyond this. I have done monstrous things – or at least Hare tells that I have. Through the whisky the remembering is not as easy as it might be.'

'So now you're innocent.'

'Oh no,' said Burke. 'I killed the Docherty woman and that's what I'll swing for. But the others? Was it me? Hare? Broggan? Constantine? Sometimes I wonder.' Burke moved closer, his upper body bent towards Rose suggesting the attitude of a confidence between friends, though he stayed far away enough to be out of reach. 'I'll tell you something, Captain Rose. I think when I killed the Docherty woman, I wanted to be caught. I hid her under the bed. Can you imagine in a crowded dossing house I hid a body under a bed that many would use? That's not a sensible plan.'

Burke chuckled again and then winced and shifted his position. 'I'm a bit more on the agony side today. Must be what is making me thoughtful. Or maybe it's something in the air. Have you got anything you want to share with me, Captain? God knows I'll be going to my grave soon enough and anything you tell me will go with me.'

'You're offering to take my confession?' asked Rose. The feeling that he was falling down a long and endless well shaft was growing. Burke waited a while, but Rose said nothing more.

'Later then,' offered Burke. 'As I was saying I decided in my total lack of wisdom to hide the body under the bed. Then I threw whisky around the room like a madman.'

'You were over-confident,' said Rose. 'You'd killed so many.'

'Welcome back to the conversation, Captain,' said Burke and clapped his hands. 'That indeed was what yon prosecutor made out. But I see now there was a part of me that had had enough. After that woman's grandchild, and I know that was me – I see his dumb, pleading, wretched face every time I lay down to sleep. But what else could I do? I killed his granddam when I was filled with the whisky and then there was this deaf and dumb child left with no protector. I swear to the good Lord himself that at that time I could see no other way for him than to send him back to the Lord to look after. He would have starved to death in the streets, frozen in the winter – why the suffering he would

51

have gone through doesn't bear thinking about. I did a terrible, terrible thing in killing him but, if I had let him live, life would have been more terrible to him than I.' Burke brushed away a tear from his cheek. 'I reckon that was the Lord's true punishment to me. To make me take the life of a child. But I was left with the choice of letting that helpless child rot on the street or taking from him a life of pain.'

'Only God has the power to take life,' said Rose. The image of Jenny rose up in front of his eyes. What would happen to her when he and Sarah were old? What if Ben or James could not, would not, care for her? What would he be prepared to do? He shook his head and pushed away the thoughts. 'You are a monster,' he spat at Burke.

Burke stood up and strode across the cell. To Rose's eyes he seemed filled with unaccustomed vigour. He punched the bricks of the wall. 'What would you say if I told you I believed God to be as careless of life as I?'

'That you are talking blasphemy,' said Rose.

Burke nodded. 'Indeed, but am I not made in God's image? He took enough of my children. Six wee innocent mites he took from me and my wife back in Ireland. He had begun to punish me before I even began and then at the end he took me to a place where I killed a child. Something even I,' he raised his voice, 'even I, in all my depravity, believe is monstrous.'

Burke stayed silent for a moment. Then his shoulders sagged and he returned to sit on the floor in front of Rose. 'You'll excuse me, Captain. But even I cannot sometimes help rail against what the good Lord has sent me.'

'You lost six children?' said Rose. 'Is this the truth?'

Burke held his gaze and nodded. His eyes were filled with tears.

'I cannot imagine,' he said.

'Aye, Captain I wouldn't want you to. I wouldn't want anyone to.'

Rose took a deep breath. The stench of the cell lodged deep in his lungs. This was the reality. This was where he was. He was not sat in a tavern somewhere discussing life with a friend. He was in the cell of a man who had killed again and again. But yet, to lose so many children would make any man question his lot in life.

'I am sorry for your loss, William. I am sorry for any man who has had to bear such a loss, but it cannot ever excuse what you did. And I think being an educated man you know this.'

'I thank you for your pity, Captain. You are indeed a good man and I think I see now what troubles you. You see me as man and you see me as a monster. You cannot hold both images in your head at the same time. That's it, isn't it? You want me to be a monster, but the more you know of me the more I show you I am also a man. And that a man could do what I have done is more than you can easily comprehend. It would be so much easier if I was only a monster with no human feelings and no tragedies in my past. But it is so much more complicated than that. And that is what causes your head to spin, is it not?'

Rose got unsteadily to his feet. He picked up the stool. 'You won't see me again,' he told Burke.

As the cell door clanged behind him, he thought he heard Burke whisper, 'Ah, but I will.'

Outside the weather had cleared and lost much of the bitterness of earlier, but Rose felt cold through to his bones. He hoped Sarah had got him another pie. He needed hot food. He needed the warmth of his family. As he passed under the shadow of St Giles, the thought sprang into his head that he had been sitting with the devil himself. It took a strong effort of his will not to seek out a priest, but he had no wish to be a town laughing stock. He ran the rest of the way home.

VII

Two guards dragged the prisoner towards the gallows. The sorry wretch sagged between them. His feet dragged along the ground. The man's entire body shook with terror. He was sobbing and, from his position marching behind, Rose would see he was soiling himself again and again.

One sallow-faced priest stood on the platform. He appeared to be exchanging a joke with the hangman, who was rubbing his hands together and stamping his feet to rid himself of the cold.

However many times he attended an execution Rose could never treat it easily. For him it was a solemn occasion. A man was being sent to meet his maker and answer for his crimes. But to the city it was a day out for all the family and to his men it was hard day of work as all the petty criminals of the city took it upon themselves to rob, loot and pickpocket while attention was elsewhere.

A man with beer on his breath, and loose teeth in his mouth, pushed forward to spit at the prisoner. Rose gave the man a hard knock on the side of his head with his cudgel. It wasn't hard enough to send him into unconsciousness, but enough to make him think again about interfering with the work of the city guard and hopefully deter any in the crowd who had been thinking of following his example.

The cold and the season had kept the crowd within more manageable limits than he had foreseen, but Rose knew that if the crowd turned ugly and surged towards the platform they might well rip the man physically limb from limb while still alive. His men had their weapons but they were outnumbered by the sheer press of people.

A pie hawker stumbled into the way of their procession, pushed by the mass of people, but quickly moved back, treading on the toes of a big man and hastily offering one of his wares in apology. Rose sensed the mood of the crowd was unsettled. There was still a holiday atmosphere, but as always there was the sheer animal delight in seeing another suffer rising to the surface. The priest, an old hand at these affairs, raised his hand and made the sign of the cross over the approaching party. The mood of the crowded settled almost at once. God had become involved and while they were more than happy to condemn the poor wretch for his crimes, they had been reminded not to sin themselves.

It took the efforts of the two guards and Rose to heave the man up to the platform. It wasn't that he was resisting them, so much as he had lost total control of his limbs. When they hauled him in front of the noose he began sobbing and crying. Rose turned away. He looked out at the crowd. A small boy rode on the shoulders of his father waving a half-eaten roll. He had an angelic face, ruddy with the cold, and he was close enough that Rose could see his eyes were sparkling with excitement. His father, a well-to-do merchant by his clothing, was keeping tight hold of his son's legs. The boy crumbled some of his roll into his father's hair and the man looked up half remonstrating, half laughing. Rose felt the all too familiar feeling of falling headlong down an endless well. His vision blurred for a moment and he felt dizzy. One of the other guards nudged him. He looked at him uncomprehendingly as the man gestured at his feet. He couldn't remember the guard's name though he had been working for him for years. He looked down and saw a puddle of piss streaming across the platform. He stepped aside.

The priest was intoning, quite loudly, over the rising sobs and screams of the condemned man. Rose forced himself to look at the prisoner. He was a short, thin scrap of a man. His age could be anywhere between twenty and forty. His thin hair was matted with the dirt of his cell. His clothes were no more than rags and barely covered him decently. There was froth at the side of his mouth and his eyes darted back and forth like those of an animal in a trap. Rose found himself sliding into a cool dispassionate state. Surely, this was the time for the man to confess, to cleanse himself before meeting his maker. Wasn't that the point of the priest? He knew that this priest was all too fond of his port and cared mostly for the extra shillings he earned for being in attendance, but to the prisoner he was the last man to be able to intercede between him and God.

Rose prided himself on being a professional. He was here to witness the actions of the law sanctified by the court process. He was the representative of law in the chaos of the Old Town. Here on the platform he was the last witness to a man's life and a reminder to all that those who broke the law would surely pay.

'But I didn't do it!' screamed the prisoner as the rough noose was slipped over his neck. 'I'm innocent.'

It was not the first time that Rose had heard these final words, but it was the first time that he had ever truly wondered if the condemned was telling the truth.

Then came the thunk of the trapdoor opening. The crowd roared and cheered. What once had been a man walking the streets of the Old Town was now no more than a snared animal dancing his last for the enjoyment of the crowd. One of the guards leaned over. 'He's still pissing,' he said. 'I wouldn't have thought he'd have so much in him.'

VIII

'Sounds like he had a reasonable crowd for his send off,' said Burke. 'Not as big as mine is assured to be, of course, but respectable. What did he do?'

Rose shook his head. 'I can't remember.'

'Dear me man, I hope you remember what my sins are when you're watching me do my final dance. A man likes to be remembered for what he did.'

'He said he was innocent.'

'And I'm sure he's the first to say such a thing,' said Burke with a spirited grin. 'Though I have to say when you're up there standing on the platform there does seem little point in protesting.' He paused. 'I've been thinking long and hard about my last moments. I don't suppose I'd be allowed to address the crowd?'

'What would you say?' asked Rose, genuinely curious.

Burke scratched his head, pulled a flea from his hair and idly cracked its back. 'Ah now, that's the question. I suppose I could thank them for coming. I expect many of them will have made quite an effort to be there. Shut up stalls early and all that. I'd like them to get their money's worth as it were. Add a bit of show to the final moments.' He cocked his head hopefully on one side. 'I could even put in a bit about not sinning as the city's fine guard would be bound to catch you. A warning from just before the grave!'

'No,' said Rose.

'Ah, well, I confess I didn't think it was likely. It would be setting an unfortunate precedent. Give all those pickpockets in the crowd a bit of extra time to do their work and the drunkards all the more time to drink.'

'No one would hear you above the crowd,' said Rose flatly.

'Do you not think they'd quiet to hear a monster like me speak?' asked Burke.

'It will not be your words they've come to witness.'

Burke looked down. 'No, I suppose not,' he said quietly. Then he shook himself and became brighter. 'Still, witnessing my death will doubtless give them a lift for the rest of the day. A bit of brightness in their dull lives.'

'How can you think such things?'

'Ah, poor Captain. You've been walking among the criminals of this city for so long, but you don't understand do you? You're a man of honour who walks the straight and narrow. Do you know how rare that is in this city? Can it be that you do honestly believe in this city's justice?'

'Of course,' said Rose.

'You probably believe in the essential goodness of a man's soul too. All I can say is the Lord has never tried you as he tries those who end up within these walls.'

'You have–' began Rose, but then he bit his lip and stopped. Then he gave a slow smile. 'You almost had me there,' he said. 'But you will not get me comparing myself to the likes of you.'

Burke's eyes sparkled in the gloom and he rubbed his hands. 'Is that so?' he said. 'You've seen men who've done terrible things. They've cursed you and spat at you. Behaved like animals without a vestige of humanity and you've been able to look down on them. I bet that in your heart of hearts – for you're not a cruel man Captain Rose, like some who work here – I bet that in your heart of hearts you felt pity. You thought they were low, no better than they should be. A breed apart from the likes of you. But then along comes I. I make jokes when others have despaired. I can debate with the best. Your men, hardened though they be, enjoy my yarns. I treat you polite. And that frightens you, doesn't it

Captain? That what you think of as evil can wear so fine a face. I'm not even dead and I'm haunting you.'

Rose sought for some retort, but the words refused to come. He closed his eyes to block everything out. Burke's voice, pleasant and friendly continued, ' But I think I can help you. If you're prepared to listen. I can tell you some things that might make the mysteries of life a little clearer. Mind, I don't say you'll like what you hear.'

Rose still sat saying nothing. His eyes were focussed into the distance. His thoughts too jumbled.

'I'll take that as a yes,' said Burke. 'When Hare sent me out to find another one – for it was always he who sent me out – when I wandered the streets and I watched, these are the people I saw: the young girl with the face painted so badly she was an affront to the customers she entreated. Ah, we had a fine bit of banter. I made such fun of her I had the street rocking with laughter, so of course she was quite safe. I'd made too much of my attention to her. But I ask you, whatever your profession, from soldier to whore, should you not take a little pride in it? In yourself? But I digress. There's the fishmonger who keeps the fresh fish on the top, but sells yesterday's catch from underneath quite happily to the matron with the young family, even though he knows it will likely make them ill. Then there is the man scurrying home with that peculiar look upon his face, of a man who's just left his mistress and is hurrying home to his wife. Or the drunken slattern, who was once a pretty whore and is now no more than a pissing pot that squats in doorways all self-respect gone, shouting obscenities at passers-by when the person she loathes most is herself. And of course there's the navies, making their way among the city's poor and destitute with a few coppers in their pockets, thinking of naught but whisky. I ask you, among that typical selection who of those is innocent?'

The silence hung heavy between them.

'Still nothing to say to me, Captain? Then let me add more. I could spot them a mile away those that'd follow my smile and my bottle. They were mine for the taking. Just as the good Lord choose to take my little ones to die, so I choose which of his children would follow me to their graves. And the power of it! Choosing who would live or die. The control. That's a heady feeling. Especially for a man who's lost as much in life as I.'

'You disgust me,' said Rose.

'And rightly so,' said Burke. 'I'm the first to admit I've done terrible things. But let me ask you, Captain, when you lock a man up for the crimes he's committed, when you know that this is his last lodging place on the way to the grave, doesn't that give you a sense of power?'

'It's not the same. It's…'

'About justice and order, I know,' said Burke. 'But don't you see it's but one step away. You don't make the decision as to who will live or die, but you catch the criminals and you know that for many of them this will mean the end of their days. You have a power.'

'It's not one I relish,' said Rose.

Burke rocked back and clapped his hands together. 'Ah, come now Captain, you're proud of your fine uniform and your position in the city. And rightly so, but what you don't understand is that you and I are only a whisper apart. You do all in the name of the city, but your actions help condemn men and women to death and imprisonment. Whether you will admit it or not you take a pride in the power you have over others. What you need to understand is that it's only one thought, one deed, and you've crossed a line. Once we killed that first shot that was us, Hare and I, over that invisible line. Once you've done something terrible, monstrous, there is no way back. What you don't yet understand is that it is so very, very easy to cross that line. Or do you? You've killed, haven't you? It leaves a mark on a man, taking a life. Only those who've joined that elite club can see it, but it's there.'

'I have only killed in the line of duty,' said Rose firmly.

'But you've seen it,' pressed Burke. 'You've seen that tiny

spark go out in a man's eyes. Extinguished that inner flame, whatever it might be, and then they are gone. All that is left is a mound of flesh and blood and guts. Nothing more. That's all we are – tiny sparks – and it's so easy to put out a spark.'

Rose was falling, falling down the long well again. A face drifted before his mind, a familiar Old Town face that he'd never see again. 'They say the marks on Daft Jamie's body show he fought for his life,' he challenged.

Burke winced as if he had been struck. 'Do you take pleasure in awakening these memories?' he asked, his face suddenly forlorn. 'But since you ask I will tell you exactly how it was.'

'I didn't ask,' Rose protested weakly, but Burke had already begun his story.

Jamie followed Burke into Hare's lodging house with a bland, friendly grin on his face. His feet were bare as usual, despite the cold, and his clubfoot gave him a curious, hobbling gait. Burke was no small man, but Jamie towered above him, a friendly giant. His floppy hair and his smile – still with all his teeth for he was only a youth despite his height – told all the world as clear as day that he was every man's friend and that each day was a singular delight to him.

'Come away in, Jamie,' called Burke, 'and tell my friend your joke. This will be the best joke you've heard in a long time, Bill.'

Jamie ducked his head as he came through the doorway and stood there looking around the dark room amiably. Hare came forward to shake his hand. Jamie's large paw engulfed and he shook Hare's hand up and down repeatedly until Hare pulled his away.

'I do believe I've seen you about the town, young man,' he said.

'That is most possible, Sir,' said Jamie politely. 'It is most possible. On a fine day I am about and truth be told I will often walk in the wet.'

'Excuse me one moment,' said Hare. Jamie only blinked and stayed where he was. Hare pulled Burke by his lapels into the furthest corner. Already the worse for the whisky Burke tottered, laughed and protested mildly.

'Hey Jamie,' he called, 'What about a wee dram? I'm sure our friend is thirsty, Bill.' Hare did his best to contain Burke in the corner, but his friend had the slitheriness of the half-cut and quickly wound his way out, still laughing. 'It's a grand joke, Bill. You have to hear it.'

Abandoning more subtle methods, Hare grabbed Burke by his ear and yanked him back. Burke gave a barking yelp of protest and laughed some more. 'Are you mad?' hissed Hare in his ear. 'He's well kent.'

'Hospitality,' roared Burke. 'Give the big man a drink.'

'I'll trouble you not to trouble yourself, Sir. I'm not one for the drink,' said Jamie.

Burke bent his head and twisted, freeing himself from Hare's grip. He staggered across the room with open arms. 'But you must,' he cried. 'A joke as choice as yours must be enjoyed with a whisky.' He got to Jamie and reached up to pat him on the cheek. 'It's a custom of our country.'

'If you insist,' said Jamie politely.

'Why then we must all have a dram to enjoy this choice moment,' said Burke. He began rummaging in the row of cups that had been left on the shelf. 'Got to make sure these are appropriate,' he muttered. 'Come on Bill. Get the whisky.'

Hare shook his head but reached under one of the beds and pulled out a bottle. Burke turned round with a flourish, holding up a big glass. 'For the big man!' he cried and blew hard into the glass, dislodging the dust which backed up into his face making him cough. 'The women folk have not been doing their cleaning,' he said and passed Jamie the glass. Then he roared with laughter for no apparent reason. Jamie obediently accepted the glass, saying nothing. Hare produced two smaller glasses for him and Burke and poured the whisky.

'Swallow it quick,' Burke urged Jamie, 'then you'll not taste it.' Jamie took a small sip and grimaced. Burke grabbed the bottle from Hare and topped up Jamie's glass. 'Here's to your fine joke!'

'Shall I tell it now?' asked Jamie.

'We must toast it first,' said Burke. 'Jamie's joke!' He tilted his glass and swallowed the whisky down in one.

'Jamie's joke,' said Hare with a marked lack of enthusiasm, but he downed the whisky all the same.

Both men looked at Jamie, who hesitantly raised his glass. Burke nodded encouragingly. Hare glared darkly. 'My joke,' said Jamie feebly and swallowed the whisky. Immediately he was sputtering and coughing. Tears ran down his face. 'Shall I tell it now?' he croaked.

'Another wee top-up to get us in the mood,' said Burke reaching for the bottle. 'Sure, hardly any of that one made it down, did it Jamie-lad? But this time you'll be getting the hang of it.'

'Not for me,' said Jamie and covered his glass with one big hand. 'Here's my joke.' He drew his shoulders back and spoke loudly. 'In which month of the year do women talk least?'

Burke nudged Hare in the ribs with the point of his elbow. 'Oh aye,' said Hare. 'I mean, I don't know.'

Jamie's shoulders slumped and he spoke slowly as if to a child. 'You have to say, "I don't know, in which month do women talk least?" That's the way riddles work. I'm sorry I should have explained it before. Shall we try again?'

'Then we have to toast again,' declared Burke, sweeping aside Jamie's hand and topping up his glass. He looked up at Jamie and said seriously. 'It's the proper way of doing things.'

'I suppose so,' said Jamie sadly.

'Remember the trick, Jamie, swallow it quick! Here's to Jamie's joke.'

'Jamie's joke,' growled Hare.

All three of them threw back the whisky. This time Jamie's splutterings weren't quite so bad. Burke grinned at him and clapped him on the back. Jamie swayed very slightly. 'There is one thing,' he said, his words not as clear as before, 'now I come to think of it, it's a riddle.'

Burke nodded knowingly. 'Very important to get these things right. Another toast!' He topped up the glasses once more. 'Jamie's riddle!' The three men drank.

Jamie sneezed suddenly. 'I think I am beginning to feel a mite unwell,' he said. 'Shall I tell it now?'

Under his breath Hare muttered, 'Dear God, please yes.'

'Indeed this is a fine time to tell it. I'll just charge the glasses so we can drink to the answer.' Once again Burke topped up each glass.

'In which month do women talk least?' asked Jamie.

'I don't know. In which month do women talk least?' asked Hare.

Jamie blinked and swayed. 'I must say, Sir, for a man no well-versed in the ways of riddles that was most finely asked.'

'Thank you,' said Hare through gritted teeth. 'Now, what's the answer?'

Jamie shook his head sorrowfully. 'Oh dear. Oh dear. We seem to have lost our way. I can't just tell you. That's wouldn't be right.'

Burke doubled up with laughter. Between bouts of hysteria he managed to say, 'Then we must begin again. I sense my friend is increasingly anxious to know the answer.'

Without being prompted Jamie upended his glass and drank down the last dregs. Then he drew himself up to his full height, threw back his shoulders and declaimed, 'In which month do women talk least?'

Slowly and carefully Hare answered, 'I don't know. In which month do women talk least?'

A smile lit Jamie's face. 'February for there are fewer days.'

An answering grin split Hare's dark face. 'That's good,' he said. 'That's very good.'

Burke, still laughing, clapped his hands. 'Certainly true of our wives, what Bill?'

'I'm glad you fine gentlemen appreciated my joke,' said

Jamie. 'I have others.'

As one man Burke and Hare retorted, 'No!'

Jamie frowned and Burke hurried across to console him. 'What I mean, dear friend, for we are all friends here, aren't we? What I dare to suggest is that you rest yourself a moment. If your other riddles and jokes live up to this fine one then you must restore yourself before your next performance.'

Jamie's eyelids flickered. 'I do feel a little tired.'

Burke took him by the hand like a child and led him over to the bed in the corner. 'Rest here, dear friend. It is very comfortable.' Jamie took him at his word and lay down. The bed was too short, so he turned on his side and curled up. He closed his eyes and very soon his breathing slowed.

Hare, standing on the other side of the room, beckoned Burke over. 'Have you calmed down now?' he hissed. 'Daft Jamie with his clubfoot is a well kent figure in the town. He'll not only be missed, but Patterson and his crew will recognise him. Besides the noise the pair of you were making on your way in here everyone will have seen.'

Burke shrugged. 'I didn't go for him in particular. I was out looking for a shot and he started talking to me. I took it as fate giving me a sign.' He patted Hare clumsily on the arm. 'And as for us being seen, why half the town is out drunk tonight. I doubt anyone remarked us.'

'He's a big lad,' argued Hare.

'Aye, but you heard him yourself say he wasn't used to the drink. Look at him, man, he's sleeping like a baby.'

'I don't like this.'

'Sure, we're having a fine time, Bill. I reckon yonder wee soul has never had such a time of it in his life.'

'It'll end badly, William.'

'Well, think on this then, Bill,' said Burke, all laughter gone, 'that's the last of our whisky in him and I've not a penny to my name. Have you?'

'Oh very well,' said Hare. 'I'll hold his legs.'

Both men gingerly approached Jamie. Burke suppressed a

giggle that came out as a short cough. Hare glared at him. Jamie gave a little snore. Hare held up his hand and counted down with his fingers. When he reached zero he threw himself hard across Jamie's legs as Burke grabbed for his face. He managed to pinch his nose, but as his hand went across Jamie's mouth their victim's eyes jerked open and he twisted violently. Jamie bit down hard on Burke's hand. Burke gave a startled cry and jumped back nursing his hand. Jamie kicked out hard and threw Hare from his legs. Hare landed on the floor with a heavy thump. Jamie, still very much affected by the whisky, staggered to his feet and called out for help. From his position on the floor Hare grabbed Jamie's clubfoot and jerked it away from beneath him. Jamie fell like a toppled tree, bashing his head on the side of one of the beds. Blood trickled down from his forehead. He gave a small child-like sob. Meanwhile Hare was doing his best to scramble on top of the fallen giant. 'William,' he yelled. 'Help me or the bugger'll get away.'

Burke, who had been cradling his hand and watching in disbelief, knelt down and made a half-hearted attempt to grab Jamie's arms. Jamie threw a punch hard at him and by more luck than skill landed one straight on Burke's nose which began to stream. Burke sat back hard. Jamie sat up and tore at Hare's head, yanking his hair and bashing his forehead off the ground. At the same time he kicked out with all his might. 'Help me!' yelled Jamie. He struggled partially free. Hare still held desperately on to one ankle. Jamie used his strong arms to pull himself along by the edges of the bed and towards the door.

'William!' shouted Hare. 'I can't hold him. Do something!'

Burke's hand found the discarded whisky bottle. He brought it crashing down on Jamie's head. Glass flew in all directions. Jamie slowed. Hare took the advantage and flipped him on to his back. Burke pinched his nose hard and covered his mouth. Blood streamed from his own nose and mingled with the blood from Jamie's forehead. The boy struggled fiercely, but Burke held on and this time Hare was not thrown off. Jamie's back bucked despite Hare's weight, foam dribbled out between Burke's fingers and tears streamed down his face but finally Jamie was still.

Burke lifted his hands first and sat back. He was breathing heavily. Jamie stayed unmoving. Finally, convinced he was dead, Hare too sat back and stared down at the body. 'The bugger,' he said softly.

Burke ripped a piece of Jamie's scarf and began to bind his hand. He looked up at the panting Hare. 'There you are,' he said, 'you'll never need to listen to his jokes again.'

Burke fell silent. He watched Rose carefully. When the captain showed no signs of speaking or moving, Burke gave a sigh and shrugged. 'Think of it as a public service, if it helps you, Captain. No one has to have their wits addled by those daft jokes.'

Rose heard himself speak as if his voice came from a long way hence. 'You're a cold man.'

'Cold, am I?' said Burke and gave a laugh that rang false. 'And what would you call yon Dr Knox? He cut off the face and feet of the body before he gave it to his students. Hare was right, Daft Jamie was a well kent figure. Him and his clubfoot. But Dr Knox is a professional gent. It couldn't be that he kent well what we have done, could it?' Burke sagged and rubbed his hand over his face. 'Ach well, it never served anyone well to think too hard on what is past.'

Rose picked up his stool and left without a word.

IX

At home Rose found his daughter up and sitting in a chair. He rushed to hug her, but was dismayed when his Jenny did not return his embrace. Little Jamie came across and patted his father on the shoulder. 'It's not you,' he said. 'She just sits.'

Sarah put down a bowl on the table with a loud clatter. 'Boys, your bread is here,' she called. Then she came over to Jenny and Rose. She bent down and gently tucked Jenny's hair behind her ears. 'It could be worse,' she said. 'It could be much more.'

'She's like this all the time?'

'No, she's a good girl,' said his wife. 'She understands us, don't you Jenny love? She's always ready to do what is asked. You just have to remind her to do things.' Sarah's voice cracked slightly. She turned away swiftly and went to settle an argument, over who had the largest piece of bread, between her two little boys. Rose stayed where he was crouching on the floor and staring into his daughter's vacant eyes hoping for some sign of recognition. There was none. He had lost her.

X

Rose slept little that night. His mind was full of questions, questions that he wanted to ask of God and that he knew he had no chance of having answered. He tossed and turned under the rough woollen blankets until Sarah, half asleep, prodded him hard in the ribs. Then he lay on his back and stared into the darkness. His imagination made shapes before his eyes aided by the dying embers of the fire. However, try as he might he could not conjure them into any form. He strained to hear his family around him. Sarah was snoring slightly. He could hear the quiet breathing of his two boys, but from Jenny, now back in her bed, he heard no sound. He wondered if she had died in her sleep and the thought came to him sudden and sharp that this would be a blessing. His eyes welled and he felt tears trickle down his face. She had been his angel and God had played the cruelest trick taking her from him, but leaving her form behind. But another part of him still did not believe that she had fully lost her wits. There was hope, he told himself. Sarah had hope and he should pray for God's help and leniency. There had to be hope while she lived. He could not help but follow the thought to Burke's actions killing the deaf and dumb child to protect him. In the lonely night he realised he not only understood, but believed in Burke's despair of having committed that crime. From there it was no long step to thinking of a man who had lost six children as young as his boys. He thought of losing James and Ben too, and felt rage surge through him. If God had done that to him he would have wanted to pull him from the sky to make him answer.

He did not fall asleep until dawn and even then his dreams were bitter.

XI

Rose woke early. He lit the fire and started the gruel for breakfast. The winter sun was still asleep and he stumbled over a stool in the half-light. Sarah sat up in bed, a sudden, jerky waking he remembered all too well from when the boys were babies and cried in their sleep. She pushed her tumbled hair from her face and rubbed her eyes. 'It's me, love,' said Rose. 'Making a start on breakfast.'

Sarah pushed the covers aside and stood. At once she snatched the top cover and wrapped it over her night gown. 'It's too early,' she said, her speech thickened by sleep.

'Slightly early,' admitted Rose, 'but I've a task to do before I start work proper.'

'What?' asked Sarah.

'Nothing for you to worry about, love,' he said. He ate quickly before the boys woke. As he gave his confused and sleepy wife a kiss on the cheek he realised he had not told her of his fear of Jenny having died in her sleep. He did not stop to check, but strode out into the watery grey light of what promised to be yet another cold, wet, winter's day.

'Am I getting out today, Your Honour?'

Hare was dirtier, smeller and even more foul than the last time Rose had seen him. He appeared to make no effort to keep any part of himself clean or tidy. Rose had seen to it that he had been provided with fresh straw and his slop bucket was cleaned out properly. He knew the guard had only complied because they feared his sudden inspection. Hare was the kind of prisoner you let rot. One of the very few Rose and, he knew, his men, felt should simply have the key turned on him and have the world walk away. And yet he would go free.

'I came to see if you had any last message for Burke.'

Hare squatted down and scratched at his balls. 'Sure it will be a release from the pain for him.'

Rose turned his face away in distaste. 'You speak as if you have no ill will against him. If it wasn't for you he wouldn't be swinging.'

Hare spat onto the floor. 'I done what I must.'

'He spoke of you and your wives as being the only ones who mattered to him in the world.'

'Well, he's lost a lot,' said Hare. 'All those kiddies back in Ireland, if you're to believe him. It's not surprising he wanted a family of his own. Cos that's what we were – family. And family sticks together.'

'As you have stuck by him!'

Hare seemed not to hear him. 'He was always right fond of Nell. Though she was a wild creature with a foul mouth on her. But then I reckon not many others would have put up with his ways.'

'The drinking?'

Hare gave a guttural wheeze that ended in a cough. Rose realised he was laughing. 'Lord love Your Honour, no. We all drank. I mean this carrying on with the wenches. Burke was always a man who needed a woman, sometimes more than one at a time, if you know what I'm meaning. Depravity by your standards, I have no doubt. But looking like he did he didn't have a lot of trouble turning the women to his ways. By the Lord, I don't reckon the man paid for it in his life and the things he could get those women to do for him.' Hare sighed. 'Whereas I had to marry the one I got just to keep her and she's a poor lot. Nell, now, she had spirit. A feisty one. I like that. I know she's beaten the rope, but I'm for thinking the mob will be after her as soon as Burke swings. Shame that. But at the end of the day a man like me has to look after himself.'

'You have no sense of honour,' said Rose.

Hare tipped an imaginary hat at him. 'Cannae afford one, Your Honour.'

'Hare is nothing like you!'

Burke rolled onto his side and sat up. He pulled his coat straight and pushed his fringe out of his eyes. 'So the ladies often remarked.'

'He is as foul and stupid a brute as he looks. A good tool for murder.'

'You've been speaking to him again, haven't you? Now what did you want to go and do that for? He'll only upset you.'

Rose sat down on his stool and waited. Burke cocked his head on one side. 'Were you hoping he'd take back his testimony?'

'I cannot rid myself of the sense that all is not yet told. One of you is lying, but I don't know which one.'

Burke sighed and shrugged. His coat fell open and Rose couldn't help but notice how very thin he had become. Following his gaze, Burke jerked the worn coat tighter around him. There was a ripping noise as the fabric at the shoulder gave. 'Damn it!' cried Burke. 'I have nothing but rags to wear on the scaffold.'

Rose said nothing. Burke played with his coat for a while, trying to work it into a better shape. Finally he gave up. 'Does it matter now?' His voice was loud and almost a shout.

'It does to me,' said Rose in a low, firm voice.

'Whatever he says now there's nothing to be done. My execution is set.'

'Yes,' said Rose. 'I am not trying to raise false hope. You will die.'

Burke's face split into a grin. 'Sure, we'll all do that. It's what makes men equal if only they'd see it.' He paused and his face grew solemn. 'Did he ask about his own wife?'

'In passing. Talking about your love of women.'

Burke's grin returned for a moment. 'Ah, the ladies. Such

beautiful creatures. A grace and a beauty and a warm place for a man to rest his cock. They alone should make one believe in God. But you noted he didn't seem much concerned over her?'

'What?' asked Rose, confused by the quick turn of subject.

'His wife.'

'No.'

'Now Nell and I might not be married in the sight of God, my having a wife back in Ireland and all, but Hare and his wife had a very different bond from the one Nell and I share. Hare loved his missus's lodging. He was a lodger there before her first husband died.'

'Are you saying he killed him?'

'Direct and to the point, Captain. Honestly, I don't know. I didn't know him then. But I'll tell you this – he took to the murdering right easy. He was the one who showed me how to do it quiet-like.'

Rose sat back and crossed his arms. 'So at the end you fling the blame on him?'

Burke rolled his head from side to side, stretching his neck and rubbing the nape. 'I chose them. I helped hold them down. I helped take their bodies for sale. I drank the whisky.' He looked directly at Rose and held his gaze. 'Yet I never harmed a hair on a living soul's head till I met Bill Hare. I might be a misguided soul, but Hare's as dark of soul as he is of looks.'

'He's an idiot,' said Rose.

'He's sharper than me for he's not hanging.'

Rose stood up. 'There's no time left.'

Burke said quickly, 'I respect you for trying to work all this out. It's more than yon prosecutor did. Hare plays the idiot, but he's smarter than many gave him credit. And I include myself in that.'

Almost against his will Rose found himself asking, 'Tell me about the first murder. Not the sick men…'

'Abigail Simpson. Hare found her. Brought her back and plied her with whisky. I recall she could fair hit the bottle.

Made her sick, but she up and took some more. Only stopped when she passed out.'

'And then?' asked Rose.

Burke shook the vomit off his shoe. It was his best pair of boots. His only pair that didn't leak in the rain. He dug under one of the beds and pulled out a bit of straw. He scraped at the mess, but all he managed to do was get it all over his fingers. He collapsed down on the bed, tugged his shoe off and threw it at the wall opposite. Abigail stopped spinning for a moment, threw back her head and laughed as if he had just made the greatest joke in the world. She took a slug from the bottle, their bottle, and started to spin again, singing in a high, warbling voice. Burke felt his hands clench into fists. He couldn't stand this much longer.

Hare sat down beside him and placed a friendly hand on his shoulder. 'It won't be much longer,' he said and winked.

Burke, who moments before had been thinking how much he wanted to ring this old biddy's neck, felt his stomach fall away. 'You're not thinking of taking her to the doctors?' he whispered. 'She's not sick.'

Hare leaned back, stretching his arm above his head. 'She's old,' he said. 'And she's no one to miss her.'

'But that's murder!'

Hare turned to face him. His black eyes twinkled. 'What did you think it was before, William-boy?'

Burke felt his guts twist inside. 'It was a mercy. The fever would have taken him. It could have taken us. We were protecting our own,' he stopped, knowing he was gabbling. Hare continued to gaze steadily at him. Burke twisted uneasily. He broke Hare's gaze and wiped his fingers across the bed. Abigail began a new verse. The high notes cut into his head. Would she never stop?

'Have it whatever way makes you content.' Hare's voice was low and conspiratorial. 'This old biddy is near her time. You and me and our women have a lot of living yet to do. It's only right the old make way for the young.'

'Only God decides when we die,' snapped Burke.

A lazy smile stretched across Hare's face. He pulled a flea from his hair. 'Guess that makes us gods!'

'Bill!'

Abigail, now forgotten by both men, continued to twirl.

'What do you want me to say, William? I know how you love your scriptures. Do you want me to say we're damned for eternity as murderers? Cos if we are what difference does one more make? Damned once or damned a hundred times, it's still damnation.'

'But the others were mercy killings,' said Burke.

Hare waggled a finger at him. 'You can't have it every which way, William-boy. You said plain and clear only God may decide when a man will die. So either we are tools of the good Lord or we're plain murderers.'

Burke sank his head into his hands. 'Dear God, we're damned.'

Hare clapped him heartily on the back. 'So one more will not be making a difference.'

Burke jerked away from him. 'I'll repent.'

'Whatever makes you happy, William-boy. Only do it while you're lying on yon drunken biddy and I'll hold over her mouth and nose. Makes it nice and easy. Quiet too.'

'I can't.'

Hare stood and faced him. Abigail continued her song, dancing behind him, oblivious to the confrontation. 'You going to stop me? I'll fight you!'

Burke gave a dry sob. 'I don't want to fight you. You're more a brother to me than my own kin.'

'Then choose between your God and your brother. Your God who took away your bairns or your brother who'll see you're never without whisky. That sweet, sweet fire that burns away all your pain.'

'Dear God help me.'

'Don't think he's listening, William-boy. I'm the one here for you.'

'I'm damned,' said Burke.

Hare pulled him to his feet. 'It'll get easier. I promise.'

'This is a nightmare.'

'Hey, Abigail old love, come over here. My brother and I want a word with you.'

'And then we killed her,' said Burke. His voice was flat and emotionless. 'I killed her. I did as he asked and lay on her while he stopped her breath. She was frail as a bird. It took no time at all. She was gone and I was well on my path to damnation. But do you know what I did after she was dead?'

'No,' said Rose.

'I laughed,' said Burke. 'I laughed because it was so easy. As Hare said, all that fuss over a moment's work.'

'I don't know what to say,' said Rose.

'Ach, there's not much you can say,' replied Burke. 'Hare knows how to reach into a man's soul. He can turn your world in on yourself before you know it.' Burke gave a little laugh. 'Only problem he has is, looking like he does folk'll rarely listen. I'm sure that's saved many a soul. Then he got me. Fair of speech and fair of face to do his work.'

'Are you saying you were under his spell?'

'Honestly,' said Burke with a shake of his head. 'I cannae tell you. He was right though. It did get easier. Once you've crossed the line to being a murderer, once you've damned yourself, how can you go back?'

'You can repent.'

'It's not enough,' said Burke. 'I need to pay the price. Lord knows my life's not worth much, but it's all I've got to give.'

'And Hare gets away free?'

Burke cocked his head to one side and looked far into the distance as if he could see beyond the damp cell walls. 'He used to say we were defying God. I could never reconcile the taking of my bairns with what I had learned about the good Lord. So for a while I was a willing convert to Hare's rejection of God. I was Hare's monster and I deserve to hang. Have no doubt about that, Captain Rose. I succumbed to temptation and to pride. It was a relief when they caught me. I was Hare's monster, but now I'm a man again. I go to meet my maker willingly.'

'You've no fear of death?'

Burke threw back his head and laughed loudly. His face lit up with mirth and for the first time Rose saw exactly why so many had followed him to their deaths. 'I'm not looking forward to the dying part. Though I don't expect it can be more painful than what the good Lord has me sitting on right now.' He sobered. 'But the death itself with be a welcome release. It will be like waking from a nightmare.'

Rose lent forward. 'You're at peace with it all?'

'You mean away from the priest and journalists? Just between us two?'

'Exactly,' said Rose.

Burke sighed. 'That one lad. The deaf mute. The whisky was in me. I never thought of what would happen to him once I killed his protector. And he knew somehow. Though he never saw a thing, I swear. He knew she'd gone. Hare was all for turning him out onto the street, but I took him across my knee and broke his back. All the time the poor dumb soul was pleading with me with his eyes, but whether he pled for life or death I could not tell you. His face haunts me day and night.' Tears trickled down Burke's cheeks. He wiped them away roughly with his sleeve leaving a stripe of dirt across his face.

'That's the first time I've seen you show remorse,' said Rose. 'You showed none at your trial.'

'I had to put on a show for the crowd,' said Burke. 'They were expecting a monster and I gave them one. There was no way out, so I thought I'd go in a blaze of infamy.' He shrugged. 'Still the sin of pride.'

Rose reached into his coat and produced a small flask. Burke's eyes fixed on it. 'Why Captain Rose,' he began.

Rose held up a finger to silence him. 'The death that haunts you is the one I understand the most.'

'I hope for your sake that's not true,' said Burke, his eyes never leaving the flask that Rose was unscrewing. Rose handed it to him.

Burke inhaled the smell, a look of bliss on his face. He held the flask high, 'Yesterday's gone and tomorrow's not ready. There's only the now and the blessed whisky. Farewell to all my friends.' He put the flask to his lips and drank deeply. He lowered the flask and returned it to Rose. He ran his tongue around his teeth and lips savouring the fading taste. 'Ah Captain Rose, you've never seemed more real to me.'

Rose took the empty flask and smiled. 'And you to me, William Burke.'

XII

Captain Rose shivered despite his heavy coat. The wind sliced through the execution site. As he had suspected, all around the platform the Lawnmarket was packed. People hung out the windows of the five-storey tenements with little regard to their own safety. Every window was open and the men leaned out waving their hats or flasks. The women clutched their babes to them and looked out wide-eyed. The noise was tremendous. Rose could discern no words clearly, but the swell of human voices jeered and cheered. The crowd below ranged from the Lawnmarket up to the Castle and down the Royal Mile, packed densely together and all baying, like wild beasts, for death. In all his career Rose had never witnessed such a spectacle of combined hate and unbridled joy. Despite the close proximity of those on the platform he felt cold deep down inside him. This was the nineteenth century, the age of civilisation and yet the people of his city massed together like some great monster sent by Satan himself to drag one soul down into hell. And there was the true problem; he cared. He knew Burke deserved his fate, but he was not a willing witness to his last moments. Rose had seen countless executions. He had seen men and women weep and wail at the last, but he had become hardened to it. Or he thought he had. This time he felt sick to his stomach and he hated the crowd. Hated them with a passion he didn't know he had.

Snow began to fall across his vision, light and swift, but he could still make out the once handsome face of the man who stood in front of him. Dirty, unshaven, with his lank dark locks falling below the collar of his ill-fitting black suit, Burke still held himself with a vestige of his former confidence though he was very pale. His blue eyes met Rose's directly and he gave a partial wink, so quick only Rose could see it. As he did, the laughter lines flashed across his face. A lesser man would have quailed before the hate of an entire city but William Burke, accused of being the most notorious serial killer the country had ever caught, relished his last moment of life. A memory flashed into Rose's mind of the first time his men dealt roughly with him; Burke had urged them to 'take care with such a historical figure'. Whatever he was and whatever he'd done, Rose saw an extraordinary bravery in this man and it made him doubt. Doubt everything,

Rose dropped his gaze to the wooden platform beneath him; the normally grubby planks scrubbed clean for the great occasion. Below this the crowd roared. Now, he could make out words like 'murderer', 'death' and all the usual abuse thrown at the condemned. The difference was the volume. A sea of humanity surged below them. Doubtless the pickpockets and ruffians were having a fine time. But Rose envied his men down there in the thick of it all struggling to keep the peace. Up here, wedged between the many clergymen Burke had invited to witness his death, it was warmer and ranker. He stood so close to the priest on his left he could see the sweat breaking out on his fat face and had all too good a view of the large black pockmarks that littered his skin.

The priest who was muttering, intoning liturgy Rose guessed, had a small smug smile lifting the corner of his mouth, obviously proud of gaining his place in history.

The hangman, an over-muscled, toothless individual, chosen for his ability to repel climbers onto the scaffold and for his apparent complete lack of compassion for his victims, pushed forward and lowered the rope around Burke's neck.

The wind changed direction and Rose felt his eyes begin to sting as the snow was driven directly at the little group.

He brushed it from his eyelashes to watch Burke's last moments; it was all he could do for him now. Burke's gaze met his and then the condemned man spoke, but the wind whipped away the words. 'I can't hear you,' shouted Rose. Burke mouthed the words again. Rose shook his head. The hangman stepped between them to lower the rope. For one wild moment Rose thought of pushing them all aside to reach his friend. His friend. He thought of Burke as a friend. His mind reeled. He stepped back. One of the priests caught his arm or he would have fallen from the platform to the surging masses below.

The hangman stepped back and Rose saw a moment of concern on Burke's face as he tried to say something to the man. The hangman shrugged and stood ready by his lever to open the trap. Rose saw it. The knot at his neck was to the side. The drop would not break his neck. The hangman had determined to give the crowd their show and make Burke dance as he struggled for his last breath. He started forward but before he had even taken a step the priest had finished and the hangman, instead of waiting for his command, had pulled the lever. The trap opened and William Burke vanished from his sight. The crowd roared. They kept roaring and Rose knew from this that William was still fighting, still kicking. His last moments on this earth a sadistic amusement to massed crowds below. It would be agony as the rope squeezed. Burke's body would twist in the wind and no matter how ready he was to die his natural functions would kick in and he would struggle. He would dance like a puppet on a string, striving for one last breath. The blood in his ears would pound. His eyes would feel as if they would explode. Rose knew it was possible they might indeed do this. The pockmarked priest was making a sign of the cross over the trap. But he was smiling. He was looking down and watching the agonies of a man's death. Rose could not. Instead he pushed his way towards the ladder and made his way down towards the cart that was waiting to take Burke's body to be dissected. The court had shown a grim irony that Burke at the very end should share the same fate as his victims.

The rungs were slippery under his boots. Snow already piled up on them. He jumped the last few steps. The cart waited in the shadow of St Giles. A man stood holding the horse's bridle tightly. The animal's eyes rolled showing white and foam flecked along its nose. Rose recognised the beast was moments from bolting. A loud cheer buffeted him. He turned to see the body swinging slowly from beneath the platform. Burke's arms and legs were still. 'Quickly,' urged Rose to the guard who stood gaping at the spectacle, 'cut him down and get him in the cart before the crowd overwhelms us.'

But before any of them could move the body fell onto the snow and lay there like a great, black, broken doll. There was another cry from above and Rose realised the hangman was taking the rope for himself, a souvenir or an investment. He shoved one of his men in the back and together they made their way under the platform. It took them only moments to reach the body, but the remaining noose around Burke's neck was already gone. Rose urged his men to hold the perimeter while they got the body away. He knew one of them had taken the noose but if his own men were so keen for a keepsake the crowd would doubtless be prepared to rip the body to shreds right here in the streets.

'Captain!' One of the priests from the platform called down, 'We need protection!'

'Let your God protect you,' muttered Rose under his breath. It was more important he got this body away before a riot began.

Normally he wouldn't have touched the body, but this time he found himself helping three of his men load what had been Burke into the cart. He felt sick as he hauled the heavy limbs, but at the same time his blood pumped in his ears as his heart quickened. 'They shan't get him. They shan't have him,' went round and round in his head. He jumped up onto the cart and urged the driver to go. The man could barely hold the reins his hands shook so much, but whether from cold or fear Rose did not know.

The cart rolled forward. Rose signalled guards to his side to escort it. The crowd, who had been converging on the platform, sent up a loud cry and began to swarm after them. The horse strained at its harness. Its head plunged up and down in fright, but the weight of the cart and the bodies in it kept the creature from bolting. Snow drove into them; the flakes almost horizontal now. The wind pushed against Rose with heavy, invisible hands. There was no way they could outrun the crowd.

Rose leaned perilously over the edge of the cart, close enough to the wheels that he could hear the crunch of the ice beneath the wood. He yelled an instruction at the nearest sergeant. The man's face displayed shock. Rose repeated his instruction forcibly and with language he would have whipped a man for using in his wife's presence. The man nodded, understanding slowly dawning, and passed the instruction along.

Guard after guard stooped, gathered snow into their palms and hurled them at the crowd. That was how Burke escaped to his final destiny at the surgeon's hall – in the wake of a giant snowball fight. Rose could not help thinking how Burke would have roared with laughter.

XIII

'It's over,' said Rose.

'So I heard,' answered Hare. 'The guards have been talking about the strangeness of it all day. Would you say it went well?'

Rose ignored the wetness of the wall and leaned his shoulders against the old bricks. He wanted the reassurance of stone, stone old before he was born. 'He had his crowd.'

Hare wiped his nose thoroughly on his sleeve. 'Did he manage to smarten himself up?'

'He got a suit. It was too big, but better than the rags he was in.'

'So I'm free now?'

'Not quite yet. The streets are far from quiet.'

Hare shuffled over and leaned in close to Rose. His breath was fouler than the cell. Rose could see his black teeth despite the gloom. 'I'm hearing how when they came to cut him up there was too much blood in him.'

Rose turned his face away in distain. 'I wouldn't know.' He pushed Hare roughly aside and made for the door. 'I thought you should know he was gone.'

Hare caught his sleeve and jerked him back sharply. 'Because we were friends, or are you preparing me for my fate?'

'Daft Jamie's mother is gathering much support to bring a private case against you.'

Hare stepped back and shook his head. 'It won't happen. The crowd's been fed and I'll be forgot.'

'I think not,' said Rose firmly.

'You think not or you hope not?' Hare laughed. He dropped his voice to a wheedling tone, 'But, Your Honour, I've been visited by serious gentlemen to determine my wits. They found I was but a poor fool. A dupe of Burke's evil genius. I'm a poor wretch who was tempted by the devil in human form.'

Rose lashed out, but Hare easily evaded him. 'Easy man. You don't want to go beating an innocent man. It would look bad on your record.' Rose said nothing. He stood, fists clenched at his sides, struggling to regain control. 'Ah now I see,' said Hare. 'He got to you didn't he?'

'I know what you are,' said Rose. Every word was an effort. He wanted nothing more than to pound this devil's smiling face. 'I know what he was.'

Hare threw himself down on the floor, half lying, half sitting. 'This I have to hear,' he drawled.

Rose remained standing. He wanted to be clear he was the one in control, but Hare's attitude was insolent at best. He took a deep breath and tried hard not to feel he was on trial. 'He was a weak man who lived for the pleasure of the moment. When he met you he'd lost his faith in God and you saw an opportunity to twist him to your bidding by offering him prosperity. By offering him revenge.'

Hare picked his nose, regarded the result, then flicked it into a corner. 'I did that? The poor ignorant fool that I am? You seem to be forgetting he chose the victims, he brought them back to the slaughter.'

'You played on how powerless he felt. You gave him the illusion of control. The power over life and death.'

'Oh, so you're saying I made him feel like a God?'

'You tempted him into evil and when the law caught up with you, as you knew it must, you cast him aside without a thought.'

Hare stretched and cracked his knuckles. Rose waited. Hare began to laugh loud. He threw his head back and roared. Rose sat down on his stool and gripped the sides. He waited for Hare to finish. He waited for him to attack. It was clear to him he was in the presence of a madman. This was the evil he had been seeking. This laughing creature was the one who had brought death to so many.

Hare hiccupped and clutched his sides. 'Oh, Your Honour, if this be not the best joke yet. Good old William. He couldn't resist one final game. Good on him, I say. What better way to spend your last few days than doing what you are best at!'

'You are a madman.'

'Possibly,' admitted Hare, 'but you've got it all wrong Captain Rose. So very wrong.' He scratched his head. 'Tell you what, seeing as you've obviously been working too hard to uncover the truth I'll tell you what happened on that final day. On,' he raised his finger warningly, 'on condition you never repeat it to another living soul.'

'I cannot conceal further crimes,' said Rose.

'Oh, there'll be no need for that. I won't be telling you of any new murders. More straightening up some details. What do you say, Rose? Do you want to finish your role as Burke's last witness? It's secrecy on the pain of whatever you hold most dear I'm asking for.'

Rose nodded.

'You're on your honour, remember that,' said Hare. 'Now here's how it was. This is what passed between us while Gray was fetching the police. We'd got the body of the Docherty woman to the usual receiver – though the damned horse wouldn't pull the cart – but we'd done it. We were back at the lodging to clear up the mess and get our stories straight.'

Beads of sweat crowded Hare's forehead. His heart knocked hard against his ribs. Burke stood in the middle of the room unmoving.

'William, we need a plan!'

Burke turned a blank face towards him. 'The horse wouldn't move, Bill. It's a sign.'

Hare felt his frustration build. He wanted nothing more than to take Burke by the neck and shake him, but he knew he didn't have the time for that. 'It was a sorry nag, William. More than halfway to the knacker's yard.'

'God warned it not to bear our sinful burden.'

Hare ran his hand through his sweaty hair. 'It was naught but a worn-out beast, William. It's gone to be shot. Even the owner said it was of no more use.'

'Another death on our hands,' said Burke and sank down onto the now empty deathbed. He sniffed. 'It fair reeks of whisky,' he commented.

Hare walked over to the crumbling wall and slammed his palm against it. He went over to Burke and shook him by the shoulders.

'Think, William, think. What is to happen?'

Burke looked up at him and his eyes were brimming with tears. 'I told the Broggan lad to sit with the body while we went for the horse, but he upped and left and Gray's woman went poking in the straw, looking for the children's stockings.' He gave a sudden shout of laughter. 'I'd have liked to see the expression on her priggish face!'

'And?' urged Hare.

'Nell offered her money. Far too much. She's no sense at all.'

'And?' said Hare giving him another shake, 'Did she take it?'

'No,' said Burke. 'Which is good, it would have bankrupted us.'

'So it's over?'

Burke nodded solemnly. 'I think indeed it is. Gray has gone for the police.'

Hare fair danced on the spot in frustration. 'I thought you meant it was all forgot!'

'No, Bill, this is the end of the road for us. It's Nell I worry for. Who will look after her?'

'William Burke, I swear I'll wring your neck myself if you don't shake yourself out of this foul melancholy and see to mending our futures.'

'There's naught to be done,' said Burke. 'Sure, it'll be a

quicker death than from the cancer for me.'

Hare got down on one knee and forced Burke to look him in the eye. 'I do not want to die, William.'

A smile broke across William's face. 'And who said you were going to my friend? I have a plan.'

'Thank the Lord for that!' cried Hare, sitting back on his haunches.

Burke laughed too. 'See, I have made you a believer!'

'Come William, time is racing – tell me your plan.'

'There isn't enough evidence to hang us.'

'Then we get off?' said Hare, a huge grin splitting his face.

Burke shook his head. 'The town will be baying for our blood. They've been calling us resurrectionists behind our backs for some time now.'

'That's a damned lie,' shouted Hare, 'we've never dug up a body. Ours are fresh!'

'You might not to be wanting to shout that about just yet, Bill,' said Burke ruefully.

'Oh aye,' said Hare. 'The plan.'

'You turn King's evidence and make it clear that Nell had nothing to do with it.'

Hare shot to his feet. 'I will not do so! I am no clipe!'

Burke raised a calming hand. 'You do this and you and your wife are away clear. Say my Nell had nothing to do with it and she's free too.' He stood up and clasped Hare's hand. 'Think on it my friend. We've had a good long run. It had to end sometime and my end is coming soon with this cancer. You know me, I'll not die easy unless I make some try at appeasing my maker. In the gaol I will have the time to repent and saving you is in part my atonement. Let me do this last thing for you, my friend.'

'I can't do this, William. You are more than a brother to me.'

Burke gripped his hand harder. 'You can and you will. Play the fool. Make me out the devil incarnate. You must admit you'll enjoy making a fool of the guard.'

Hare gave a wry smile. 'That would be a sweet joy but no,

William, there must be another way. I am not ready to lose you my friend.'

'But I am ready to die, Bill. Do me the one last favour and respect my choice.'

Fists beat upon the door. 'Open up! Open up in the name of the King!'

'This one last act of friendship for me, Bill. Let me go.'

Hare pulled Burke to him in a great hug. Then released him and called, 'Here! Here! The murderer Burke is here!'

'So there you are, Your Honour, that's exactly how it was. Burke was my good friend until the end. And you are his last dupe.'

Rose opened his mouth to protest. But the thought that this was all too possible with Burke entered his head and he could not shake it. So, with no final word, he left Hare's cell for the last time.

That night he lay awake until he heard Sarah's sudden lament that Jenny's spirit had fled her body. Whatever Hare had told him he knew he understood Burke better. Now more than ever.

THE END

More books from Fahrenheit Press

Black Moss by David Nolan

In April 1990, as rioters took over Strangeways prison in Manchester, someone killed a little boy at Black Moss.

And no one cared.

No one except Danny Johnston, an inexperienced radio reporter trying to make a name for himself.

More than a quarter of a century later, Danny returns to his home city to revisit the murder that's always haunted him.

If Danny can find out what really happened to the boy, maybe he can cure the emptiness he's felt inside since he too was a child.

But finding out the truth might just be the worst idea Danny Johnston has ever had.

"As one would expect from a writer with the skill and experience of David Nolan, this haunting book deals with very difficult issues in an incredibly sympathetic manner while at the same time throwing a light onto one of the most complicated and shaming areas of our society - the failure to protect those who are the most vulnerable."

Rubicon by Ian Patrick

Rubicon has recently been optioned by the BBC with a view to making a 6 episode series.

Two cops, both on different sides of the law – both with the same gangland boss in their sights.

Sam Batford is an undercover officer with the Metropolitan Police who will stop at nothing to get his hands on fearsome crime-lord Vincenzo Guardino's drug supply.

DCI Klara Winter runs a team on the National Crime Agency, she's also chasing down Guardino, but unlike Sam

Batford she's determined to bring the gangster to justice and get his drugs off the streets.

Set in a time of austerity and police cuts where opportunities for corruption are rife, Rubicon is a tense, dark thriller that is definitely not for the faint hearted.

'A sharp, slick, gripping and compelling novel'

Hidden Depths by Ally Rose

In East Germany in the spring of 1989, 14-year-old Felix Waltz escapes from a life of abuse at the notorious Stasi youth prison, Torgau.

On New Year's Eve 2004, a woman awakens from a coma. She's been unconscious for 12 years since being viciously attacked by a lake. As her case is re-opened it soon transpires the events of that night are linked to events that happened before the fall of the Berlin Wall.

Hanne Drais, a criminal psychologist working with a Berlin police team, is one of those involved in reopening the case. As Hanne discovers the truth she's shocked to find both her past and her destiny are indelibly interwoven with the man at the heart of her investigation.

"A real page turner. Gripping and full of suspense with surprising twists and turns throughout, it had me hooked from the start…"

Burning Secrets by Ruth Sutton

It's the spring of 2001 and Foot & Mouth disease is raging across Cumbria.

Twelve-year-old Helen Heslop is forced to leave her family farm and move in with relatives in a nearby town because the strict quarantine means she can't travel back and forth to school in case she inadvertently helps spread the disease.

As the authorities and the local farming communities try desperately to contain the outbreak, tensions run high and everyone's emotions are close to the surface.

And then Helen disappears.

The police search expands all over the northwest coast where farms are barricaded and farming families have been plunged into chaos - not least the Hislop family, where potentially explosive fault lines are exposed.

Under the strain tensions build inside the police team too, where local DC Maureen Pritchard is caught between old school DI Bell and new broom DS Anna Penrose.

Will Helen survive? And can life for the Heslop family ever be the same, once burning secrets are discovered and old scores settled?

"During the awful Foot & Mouth emergency of 2001 many individual lives were changed forever. Burning Secret is about some of those. At the heart of the book are innocents, threatened by events they could neither prevent nor control, and those who try to protect them..."

Printed in Great
Britain
by Amazon